CW00404910

Desperate Measures

By Stephen Leather

All Malee wanted was a better life for herself and her son. And the only way she could make that happen was to sell her body, to exchange sex for money.

But her plan falls apart when she arrives in London at the start of the Covid pandemic.

She risks everything to support her family - but as the country goes into lockdown she runs into Russian gangsters who have their own plans for her.

Before long the Russians are forcing her to work for them. If she refuses, they'll kill her. Now it's not about working for a better life - now it's a matter of survival.

ALSO BY STEPHEN LEATHER

Pay Off, The Fireman, Hungry Ghost, The Chinaman, The Vets, The
Long Shot, The Birthday Girl, The Double Tap, The Solitary Man,
The Tunnel Rats, The Bombmaker, The Stretch, Tango One, The
Eyewitness, Penalties, Takedown, The Shout, The Bag Carrier,
Plausible Deniability, Last Man Standing, Rogue Warrior, The
Runner, Breakout, The Hunting

Spider Shepherd thrillers:
Hard Landing, Soft Target, Cold Kill, Hot Blood, Dead Men, Live
Fire, Rough Justice, Fair Game, False Friends, True Colours, White
Lies, Black Ops, Dark Forces, Light Touch, Tall Order, Short Range,
Slow Burn, Fast Track

Spider Shepherd: SAS thrillers:
The Sandpit, Moving Targets, Drop Zone

Jack Nightingale supernatural thrillers:
Nightfall, Midnight, Nightmare, Nightshade, Lastnight, San Francisco
Night, New York Night, Tennessee Night

Chapter 1

Sunday March 1. Today I slept with a man for money for the first time. He was an American called Tim and he was thirty-five years old, exactly ten years older than me. Am I a bad girl? I don't think so. I just want to do what is best for my parents and my son. Tim was nice to me and he stayed for two hours which cost him £300. He spent the first hour talking and then he got on top of me and I closed my eyes and he came really quickly. He kept asking me if I liked it and I lied and said that I did but as soon as he went I started crying and now I've been crying all night. I have met two of the girls who work for the agency that I work for and they both say that the work is easy and it's money for nothing. They both earn more than £3,000 every week. Every week! Can you believe that? In Thailand a teacher works for a month for about 20,000 baht, which is about £500. It would take a teacher almost a year to earn £6,000 but these girls can earn that in two weeks. I want to build a house in my home town and I want to buy a truck for my father and a nice car for myself. And I want to take care of my son. That's my plan. It wasn't my plan when I came to London. I was going to be a student and work in a restaurant and I did that for three months but now I'm an escort girl, a girl who sleeps with men for money. That's why I'm so sad and why I am crying. I never thought I would be a prostitute, but that is what I am. Am I a bad girl?

Chapter 2

Monday March 2. I cried all day yesterday. I'm not sure why I was so upset. The customer that the agency sent me was a nice man and he didn't hurt me and I made £300 for just two hours. Well, £200 for me and £100 for the agency. But I felt so dirty. I showered five times and still I didn't feel clean.

Oliver is the man who runs the agency and he phoned me at midday to say that he had another customer for me. Oliver is Vietnamese but he has been in London for a long time and speaks with an English accent and says 'innit' a lot. I couldn't stop crying and I said I couldn't work. He said that was okay but that I had to take the agency's share of the money I had earned to a flat in Sloane Square at ten o'clock at night. He said I had to do that every Sunday. I said I would try but after I hung up the phone I started crying again.

At eleven o'clock at night my son phoned me. He is only five years old so my mum helped him make the call. His name is Ice because when I was pregnant with him I ate a lot of ice. I tried not to cry while I was talking to him but he kept asking me what was wrong. I told him that I had a stomach ache.

Oliver called me at midnight and asked me why I hadn't brought him my money and I said I was too sad and that I couldn't leave my room. He banged down the phone.

At one o'clock in the morning Cat came to my flat. Cat is Oliver's girlfriend. She is Thai like me. In fact she is from Udon Thani, the same as me, but I never knew her in Udon Thani. Cat is older than me, about thirty-three or thirty-four, but she's quite pretty.

Cat was angry but she smiled all the time. She said that it was up to me if I worked or not. She wasn't going to force me and neither was Oliver. But she said that if I wanted to make money I would have to do the job. If I went back to the restaurant where I used to work then I would make very little money.

I hate what I have to do, but now I'm trapped because Oliver lent me the money to pay my rent on the flat in Bayswater where I stay. I had to pay for two months and give them one month's deposit so I had to pay £5,400 and that was money I didn't have. I have to pay him back and the only way I can earn that much money is to work for the agency. Oliver also paid £200 for the photographs on the agency's website and he said I had to pay him back. And I borrowed money from Cat to pay for the uniforms and underwear that I wore for the photographs. They cost £550. That means I have to pay Oliver £6,150. If I do not work for the agency then I cannot pay back the money I borrowed. I am trapped. Cat asked me what I wanted to do and I said that I would start working again today. Now I am waiting for Oliver to phone and tell me if I have a customer. And I am crying.

Chapter 3

Tuesday March 3. Oliver sent me a customer at one o'clock in the afternoon. He was a man in a suit and he had one of those earphone things that you use to talk on your phone with. It's funny because when he had sex with me he took off all his clothes but kept the phone thing in his ear. He told me his name was John but when I was in the bathroom I heard him on the phone and he said his name was Alistair. He called me Annabelle but that isn't my real name, it is the name the agency uses. My real name is Malee which means jasmine in Thai. He stayed for one hour and he had sex with me three times and he paid me £150. I felt sad but this time I didn't cry.

I had a shower and drank some orange juice to get the bad taste out of my mouth and then the phone rang. It was Oliver and he had another customer for me, a man called Simon, and he had booked me for three hours starting from four-thirty. I couldn't understand why a man would want to have a prostitute for three hours. Most men can only have sex for a few minutes before they come, so why did he want to spend so much time with me? I phoned Cat and asked what she thought. She laughed. She said it wasn't the sex that he really wanted, he wanted a girlfriend. He wanted someone to like him and to spend time with him. She told me that I had to pretend that I was his girlfriend then he would be happy and he would come back and see me many times. Cat is very clever, she has been in this business for a long time. She said that I wasn't a prostitute, I am an actress and my room was a stage. I was giving a performance. And if it was a good performance then the customer would come back many times. That was why Alice makes so much money, she said. Alice is the hardest working girl at the agency and customers keep coming back to see her. You have a choice, she said. You can see two different customers each day, every day. Maybe fifteen customers a week. Sixty a month. Or you can get yourself regular customers who keep coming to see you. If they like you they'll start seeing you for four or five hours or maybe even see you overnight which means they have to pay £1,100. You might only see one customer a day but you would make a lot of money. Cat made a lot of sense.

I spent a lot of time putting on sexy make-up and wearing a sexy bra and suspenders and stockings. When Simon came I kissed him on the lips and gave him a drink and then sat on the sofa and talked. He was forty and okay-looking but going bald which I don't like.

It was so easy. Cat was right. Simon wanted a girlfriend, he didn't want a prostitute. We talked about his job (he works in a phone shop), his wife (he married when he was young and doesn't love her any more) and his car (he has a Jaguar and he loves it more than his wife.) We talked for an hour and then I sat on his lap and kissed him and then I took his hand and led him to the bedroom. I undressed him and made love to him. He lay on his back and I did all the work and I pretended to come, calling his name and shivering. Afterwards I lay in his arms and he talked and I listened. Before I knew it his three hours was up. I had earned £450 of which I get to keep £300. When he left I kissed him on the lips and said that I hoped he would come back to see me and he said that he would. I don't think I will cry tonight.

Chapter 4

Wednesday March 4. The boss of the language school I go to phoned me up today to ask why I hadn't been in this week. His name is John and I think he wants me to be his girlfriend. He always closes his door when I go to his office and once he asked if he could kiss me. I know he is married because there is a photograph of him with his wife and daughter on his desk. I have to be nice to John because he helped me get my visa to come to the UK. If I want to go back to Thailand while I have the student visa then I need a letter from the school saying I have a holiday. I told John that I wasn't feeling very well and that I would try to get in on Thursday or Friday. I am supposed to go for English lessons every morning, starting at 10am but since I started working for the agency I have been too tired.

Cat phoned me to say that someone had posted a review of me on a website. The review said that I was pretty but not very enthusiastic. I think it was the man with the headset. I told Cat that the man wasn't fair because most of the time he had been talking on the phone and that I had done everything he wanted. Cat said not to worry but that the reviews were important because customers looked for girls who had good reviews. She asked me how many towels I had and I said about three. She said I should go out and buy more towels. Every time a customer comes to the flat I should give him a clean towel, and then I should give him a fresh towel when he goes to the bathroom. That means two towels per customer. Cat said I should have at least ten towels in the flat but the more the better.

Oliver sent me a customer at six o'clock. He was a painter, I think, because he came in overalls that were splattered with paint. He had his head shaved and was a bit fat, and didn't seem to want to talk at all. I offered him a drink but he said no and then I sat next to him in the sofa but he didn't want to talk. He said he wanted to go to the bedroom and when I asked him to shower he said no, he didn't want to shower. He didn't smell good but I tried to smile. Afterwards he got dressed and left without saying anything. I cried after he had gone. He treated me like a prostitute and that made me feel bad.

I went to sleep at eleven o'clock so that I could get a good's night sleep but Oliver rang me at two o'clock in the morning and said that a customer would be coming at two-thirty and that he would be staying for two hours. I wanted to say no but two hours meant £300 which is a lot of money. I showered and put on my make up and put on my stockings and suspenders. The customer's name was Ronald and he was about my age, twenty-six. He wore a suit and a Rolex watch and was quite handsome. He told me that he worked for a stockbroker and that he had just done a big deal. He took cocaine and asked me if I wanted some and I said I didn't. He wanted sex for the whole two hours. In every position. The only time he stopped was when he was taking more cocaine. I was so sore but I didn't complain. When his two hours were up he showered and got dressed and tipped me £100. I couldn't believe it. I squealed and kissed him.

He asked me if I invested my money and I said I was saving it to take back to Thailand. He laughed and said there was no point in leaving money in the bank. He asked me if I had heard of the China virus, the Wuhan Flu. He meant Covid. I knew about Covid because some people had died of it in Thailand before I flew to London. He said that Covid was coming to Europe and it would change everything. He said I should buy shares in a company called Zoom because people would talk to each other online, that I should buy shares in Amazon because people would be scared to go to real shops. And he talked about something called 'shorting' which I didn't understand but he said I should short airlines and travel companies. I smiled and said yes, okay, I would, but I won't because I do not want to take any risks with my money.

By the time he had gone it was five o'clock in the morning. I wanted to phone Ice in Thailand and tell him how much I loved him but he would have been at school so I went to sleep. I didn't wake up until John rang me. I am still tired now but I have to get ready for my first customer.

Chapter 5

Thursday March 5. I had to buy condoms today. I bought a pack of twelve on Saturday but I've used them already. I went to a pharmacy near to my flat and bought thirty-six condoms, three packets of twelve. I was so shy. The man who served me was an Indian and he was grinning. He said 'Sawasdee krup' which is Thai for hello but I pretended not to understand what he was saying.

He asked me if I wanted to buy some facemasks because he had just had a delivery. I asked him why I would need a facemask and he said because of Covid. But I said there was no Covid in England. He said I was wrong, he said that a woman had died of it in Reading which is near London. He said he had a cousin who worked in China and he said that hundreds of thousands of people had died of Covid but the Chinese Government was burying them in mass graves and lying about it. He said I should buy facemasks and hand gel and latex gloves but I said I didn't need them.

I bought lots of shower gel and shampoo and they had some scented candles so I bought some of them, too. I walked down Edgware Road and found a shop that sold towels and I bought ten fluffy white towels. In all I spent more than a hundred pounds. London is so expensive.

I only had one customer yesterday. When Oliver phoned me he said that it was probably because I had a bad review. He said that because I was a new girl customers would look at review sites to see if I was any good and if the only review was a bad one then they might not come to see me. My review was on a site called Punternet and Oliver said a lot of customers used that site. He said I should try really hard to make my customers happy so that they will say good things about me.

I never thought I would do this job. I always thought I would meet a good man in Thailand and be his wife and have children and live happily ever after. But I suppose life isn't a fairy story, is it? Life is real and sometimes we have to do things we don't want to. I have a son but I don't have a husband. He left me when I was pregnant and has never seen his son. And now I am far away from Ice, doing what I have to do to make money. I won't do this job for ever, I'm sure of that. I think I can make maybe £100,000 profit in one year and that's more than four million baht which is a lot of money. I will do it for one year then I will stop. I know Ice misses me but he is only four so he doesn't really understand. I love him so much. More than anything.

When I first came to London I went to school every day and worked in a Thai restaurant in Camden in the evenings. I made £80 a day working and I had a small room in a house near the restaurant and I went to an English language school in Hampstead. I made enough money to live on but I didn't make a profit. I was able to send a little money back to Thailand, but not much. Then I met Sandra in the restaurant and my life changed.

Sandra has long hair and big breasts and dark skin. That isn't her real name, it's her working name. Her real name is Sai. She's from Surin, in the east of Thailand. She had a good-looking English boyfriend who drives a red Porsche. They came into my restaurant and she talked to me, asking how old I was and where I was from. The second time she came in was about a week later and this time she kept talking about money, about how expensive London was and how it was impossible to save money if you worked in a restaurant. She had a lovely Louis Vuitton bag and Gucci sunglasses and Prada shoes and a lovely dress that she said had cost her £400.

I asked her what job she had and she said she worked for an agency. I didn't understand at first and I thought she meant a travel agency. Sandra and her boyfriend laughed. Then she told me about the agency she worked for. I thought she was joking but she gave me a card which had the agency's website on it and said I should have a look at it.

The next day I checked out the website on my phone. I was so shocked. There were twelve girls on it wearing very sexy clothes. The website said that some of the girls were Vietnamese or Chinese but to me they all looked like Thais. Sandra kept coming back to the restaurant and telling me how pretty I was and how much money I could earn. She said that I could go and talk to her boss and he'd tell me about it. I was stupid earning £80 a day serving food, she said, when I could earn so much more doing what I would normally do for free with my boyfriend. I thought about it for a long time before I decided to go and see Oliver. I didn't want to have sex for money but I have to take care of my son and my family.

The last customer on Wednesday came just before midnight and he stayed for two hours. He had been drinking and as soon as he came into my flat he asked if I could give him a beer. He ended up drinking three beers. His name was Andrew and he worked in an office. He wore a nice suit and a tie with rabbits on it. He made love to me in the bedroom then he asked me if I had any sexy movies. I didn't but I said I had Netflix so we watched a horror movie. I almost fell asleep but he kept touching me and kissing me on the neck. When the movie finished he wanted to make love to me again but his two hours was up. He said that was okay and that he'd pay for another hour. I phoned Oliver and asked him if that was okay and he said of course. Andrew gave me another £150 and we went back into the bedroom. He wanted me on top and I did that and pretended to come, then I lay down on top of him and said 'thank you'. I could see he was pleased. He grinned and stroked me and called me his baby. I kissed him on the lips when he left. He had paid me £450 and £300 of that was for me.

Chapter 6

Saturday March 7. My boyfriend called me yesterday from Thailand to talk about my house. Well, it's our house really. And he's my ex-boyfriend. He works in a car showroom in Udon Thani, selling Toyota cars and trucks. He's a manager and has a good salary. He also has a wife and two children. He's the reason I'm in London. It's a long story.

His name is Kung and he's old. He's fifty next year. His wife is thirty-five. I was his Mia Noi, his second wife. He helped take care of me and my son, and came to see us several times a week. Sometimes he would tell his wife that he was going to Bangkok on business and he'd stay at my house. It was a really small house, just two small bedrooms, and he said he would build a house with me. He arranged a loan through his bank and we paid every month, half-half. We hired an architect and a builder and spent ages talking about the home we were building. We had a plan. We were going to build the house and then he would leave his wife and live with me and Ice.

I have known Kung for four years and I was his Mia Noi for three years. Then his wife found out. She told Kung that if I didn't leave Thailand she would have me killed. He believed her. Her uncle has killed people before. He went to prison once for seven years for shooting a local politician and isn't scared of anyone. Kung said that I had to leave and that he would help me.

I applied for a visa to study English in London and Kung acted as my sponsor. He has a friend in the embassy and it was easy. That's why I left Udon Thani and why I left my son. Kung still goes to see Ice and he helps to take care of him. My mother went to a fortune teller and the fortune teller said that Kung will never marry me. When I left I told Kung it was better that we finished because I would be away for at least a year but he cried and said that he loved me. I don't think he does. If he really loved me he'd leave his wife and live with me and Ice, wouldn't he?

Kung called to say he needed money to pay the builders and that the bank loan payment was due. He kept asking me when I could send him money and I said soon. He kept saying that he loved me and missed me but he kept asking me for money, too.

When I hung up there were two messages from Oliver on my phone. He had a customer for me at four o'clock this afternoon. His name was Nick and he was very handsome. He was about my age and had a great body. I smiled and kissed him a lot but all the time I was with him I was thinking about Kung and the money. I wasn't sure when I could send him any. I had to pay Oliver what I owed him.

Nick wanted sex really quickly and then he asked me to give him a massage. He lay face down and closed his eyes and I spent the last half an hour of his time rubbing his back and shoulders. He was wearing a wedding ring. I felt sorry for his wife. Why couldn't she do for him what I was doing? He was handsome so I am sure he had a pretty wife. He should have been with her and not with me.

After Nick had gone, John phoned from the school to ask how I was. I said I was still a bit sick. He asked if he could come around to see me and that he'd bring some fruit with him but I said no, I was going to sleep. I said I would go to school next week. I am sure he wants to have sex with me. Why do so many married men want to have sex with other girls? Why do they get married if they want to be butterflies? That's what we call men who have lots of girlfriends. Like butterflies, they fly from flower to flower.

Nick was the only customer I saw so I only earned £150 and £50 of that is for Oliver. If no more customers come tonight then I will go to sleep early. Tomorrow is Sunday so even if I get up early the school is closed. I haven't been to school for more than a week now. But I am practising my English by talking to my customers, so that's good. I hope I get another customer tonight.

Chapter 7

Sunday March 8. I had one customer today. He came at just after eleven o'clock at night and he was so drunk that he fell into the flat. He was quite young, younger than me I think, and he had shaved his head like a monk and had an ear-ring in one ear. He had funny tattoos on his hands. On the knuckles of one hand he had 'HATE' and on the other hand he had 'LOVE'. When he phoned me about the booking Oliver told me that his name was James but when he was in my flat he said his name was Vince. I don't know why customers lie about who they are because I don't care. So long as they pay the money I don't care. He was so drunk I could hardly understand what he was saying. I asked him for the money first. Cat said I should always do that because sometimes customers didn't have money and they would try to have sex for free. Vince had a big roll of £50 notes in his pocket and he gave me three. He saw me looking at all his money and he laughed. He said did I want to know where he got all the money from and I said okay and he laughed again and said that he could tell me but then he'd have to kill me. He was joking but I didn't understand the joke. I wanted to tell him that I had more money than him but I didn't. It's best not to tell people how much you have because you might make them jealous or they might try to take it off you. I have hidden my money in the kitchen, in the drawer where I keep my knives and forks and spoons.

I asked Vince to shower but he said he didn't want to and he took off all his clothes and lay down on the bed. I was wearing my pink nightdress over stockings and suspenders and looked very sexy, but by the time I had taken off my nightdress he had fallen asleep and was snoring. I shook him but he wouldn't wake up. I lay down next to him. After an hour I shook him really hard and he woke up. He asked me if we had had sex and I said sure, it had been great, and he got dressed and went. He could barely walk. It was so funny. I wish all my customers were like Vince.

Oliver said that Sunday is always a quiet day because all the married customers are at home with their families and the ones that are single usually spend all their money on Saturday nights. I woke up early and phoned Ice and talked to him for more than an hour on FaceTime. Ice kept asking me when I was going home and I didn't know what to say. I miss him but I need money and the longer I stay in London the more money I'll earn.

I spent the morning sorting out my money. Since last Sunday customers had paid me £2,100. Of that I get to keep £1,400 and I have to give Oliver £700. And I got £150 in tips. So in one week I have earned £1,550. I can't believe it. I would have to work in the restaurant for a month to make that much money. I know Oliver will want me to give him most of my money to pay back what I owe him, but I still feel rich. I put the money down on the bed and counted it again and again. I put Oliver's money in one envelope and my £1,150 in another envelope. I put the £150 in my purse. I wasn't going to tell Oliver about the tips.

At lunchtime my phone rang. I thought it was Oliver sending me another customer but it was Sandra. She said she and a girl called Nancy were going to go to Chinatown to eat and then buy sexy underwear and did I want to go with them and I said sure.

Nancy is young, about nineteen I think. She is from Korat and is quite dark and has really large breasts. Actually she is a bit fat. Her real name is Noy. She has a very loud laugh but she never smiles with her eyes. We went to Chinatown and ate dim sum and noodles and then we went to a shop called Ann Summers which sold underwear, sexy movies, and sex toys.

I bought a lot of underwear because it was much cheaper than the shop that Cat had taken me to when I first said I would work for the agency. Sandra said that Cat got a commission from the shops that the girls used to buy their clothes and underwear, and from the photographer who took the pictures for the website. I don't think Sandra likes Cat very much.

Chapter 8

Monday March 9. The flat where we had to meet Oliver was in Sloane Square. We are all to go to the flat every Sunday night with the agency's money. Cat was already there when Sandra and I arrived, and there were another five girls with her. Cat was cooking Thai food in the kitchen. Pad Thai, Khao Pad, fried chicken and slices of watermelon. Sandra and me were the last to arrive. Nancy was there and she looked a bit drunk. The other girls were Alice, Wanda, Candy, and Vicky. They all smiled at me and said hello but I could see that they were all weighing me up. I suppose we are in competition and the prettiest girls will get the most customers. Sandra is pretty but had very dark skin. Nancy was young but a bit fat and had really big breasts which she says are real but which I think are implants.

I had met Alice before with Sandra once. She is very sexy but she had tattoos which I don't like and she is always smoking. Wanda is fairly pretty but she has crooked teeth so she keeps her lips together when she smiles. Candy is pretty but she's a bit too thin. Vicky is almost forty, though she looks a lot younger and has a really good body. But I think I am the prettiest. I could see from the way that the other girls were looking at me that they thought I was the prettiest, even though I had deliberately not worn make up and was wearing my hair tied back in a pony tail. I know I'm pretty but I also know that sometimes people can be jealous.

When we were all in the flat Cat telephoned Oliver and after fifteen minutes he arrived. He had brought some beer and some bottles of Thai whiskey and brandy. We all handed our money over in envelopes and on the envelopes we had written how much was inside. My £700 was the smallest, and it was for eight days when everyone else was giving him their money for seven days.

The girl who gave the most was Alice. She gave Oliver £2,100 which meant that she had earned £6,300 during the week and she gets to keep £4,200 for herself. The next biggest was Nancy. She gave

Oliver £1,800. Oliver put all the envelopes on the table and one by one he opened them and checked the money inside. I have never seen so much money in one place. There were seven girls and I think in total Oliver got about £9,000. Can you believe that? He got £9,000 for one week. I could buy a house in Udon Thani for that.

After Oliver had counted the money and put it in a briefcase, Cat brought in the Thai food and we ate and watched Thai soap operas on the internet. When we'd eaten the girls started playing cards. They played like crazy. They started playing at midnight and they were still playing when I went home at five o'clock in the morning. Alice lost more than £2,000. I couldn't understand that. She must have slept with loads of men to make her money, yet she was throwing it away by gambling. The girls kept asking me to gamble but I said no. I said I didn't like gambling but the real reason was that I had worked hard for my money and I didn't want to lose it. I was going to send most of what I'd earned back to my mum because I had to pay Ice's school fees for next term. That was why I'm doing this. For my son. Ice is so handsome and so smart and I love him more than anything. I phone him almost every day and he tells me how much he misses me and how much he wants me to go back to Thailand. Sometimes I cry myself to sleep because I miss him so much.

I went home with Nancy. She stays in an apartment close to mine, close to Bayswater Tube station. I didn't want to sleep alone so I spent the night at her place. She had drunk a lot of whiskey at the flat in Sloane Square. Nancy said the flat in Sloane Square is where Vicky works. No one knows where Oliver and Cat live. Nancy said she wasn't sure if that was their real names. I asked Nancy what had happened to the other girls, the ones who were on the website but who hadn't gone to the flat. I was the thirteenth girl on the website but there had only been seven girls at the flat. Nancy laughed and said Oliver didn't take a girl's photograph off the website when she stopped working for the agency. If a customer rang up and asked for a girl who wasn't working any more, he would lie and say that she was on holiday and recommend one of the girls who was working. Most customers just wanted sex and didn't really care which girl they saw. One of the girls on the website had left more than a year ago, she said.

While the girls were playing cards in the flat, Oliver took me to one side and asked me how much I could pay him back. He and Cat had

loaned me £6,150. I asked him if it would be okay to pay him back
£500 and he said he wanted more. I said that I only had £1,150 and I
had to pay for a lot of things for my flat plus £20 every day for my
mobile phone. Oliver said it wasn't his fault and that if I only paid him
back £500 a week it would be almost three months before I had paid
back all the money that I owed him. Three months was a long time, he
said. He couldn't wait three months. I asked him if £700 would be all
right but he said no, he wanted £1,000. I almost cried but I knew he
was right. He had loaned me the money and I should pay it back as
quickly as possible. But if I gave him £1,000 I wouldn't be able to
send any money back to Thailand. It was as if I had worked for the
whole week for nothing. There was only one way I would be able to
pay Oliver back and send money back to Thailand. I would have to
work harder and that means sleeping with more men.

When I first started working for Oliver I only did incall, where the
customer comes to me. But Cat taught me how to visit hotels. You
have to be confident as if you are staying there, and you have to walk
straight to the lift as if you are going to your room. If you are dressed
well and have an expensive handbag, no one will stop you. I'm glad I
started to do outcall. I get more money and I'm getting more
customers. I feel really confident now. I can walk into any hotel with
my head held high. I smile at the porters and the people at reception
and they always smile back. Sometimes after I've done a job I go to
the hotel bar and sit and have an orange juice. People always smile at
me. I think it's because I'm young and pretty. Most of the people you
see in hotel bars are quite old. Most of the outcall customers are quite
old, too. Usually more than forty.

Chapter 9

Friday March 13. People in England seem to be getting more worried about Covid now. There are almost six hundred cases they said on the TV. They said that anyone who had a cough or a fever should stay home for seven days. I had a bit of a cough but I don't think I have Covid.

I had only one booking yesterday, for one hour. His name was Peter, at least that was the name that he used when he booked me. After we'd had sex he said that his name was really David and that he wanted to be my boyfriend. He was quite good-looking and he had a good heart but I told him that I didn't want a boyfriend, I just wanted customers. He said he'd take me to the movies or to dinner or we could just go shopping. I said that we could do all that but he had to book me through the agency first. He seemed to get a bit angry then and he left. Cat warned me that a lot of customers would want to be my boyfriend because they want free sex. She said that Oliver would get very angry if he found out that I had a boyfriend, especially if it was a customer. Oliver worked very hard to make the agency a success so it wasn't fair to steal customers from him. I said that I would never do anything like that. I didn't come to London because I wanted a boyfriend. I had two boyfriends in Thailand and they didn't work out, and the last thing I wanted was another boyfriend. All I want to do is to make enough money to take care of myself and my family.

No other customers came to see me yesterday. I am not so busy now because Sandra and Nancy are working again. Sandra rang me for a chat and she told me that she had lied to Oliver about having her period. She just wanted two days off so that she could have fun with her boyfriend. I don't want to lie to Oliver, I just want to work hard and pay back the money that I owe him so that I can start sending money back to Thailand.

Chapter 10

Monday March 16. Yesterday I went to the Sloane Square flat with Nancy at just before ten o'clock. Three of the girls were already there – Alice, Sandra and Wanda. Alice had £2,300 for Oliver, Sandra had £1,900 and Wanda had £1,700. Nancy had £1,200 and I had £1,100. That was a lot more than my first week and Cat told all the girls that I was doing really well. Alice laughed and said that she had earned more than twice as much as me. I just smiled. Alice is always the best earning girl. Cat said it's because she is really good at sex and is happy to do anal. Englishmen like anal, she said.

I haven't spoken to Alice much. She's pretty and has long hair but she has a lot of tattoos which I think is a bit scary. Wanda told me that Alice used to work in a pool bar in Bangkok and that she slept with men for money, mainly farangs, which is what we call foreigners. I never slept with men for money in Thailand. I could never do that. I'm not a bad girl. I'm only doing it in London because I want to make a lot of money quickly. This week I earned £3,300. I had seventeen customers. Fourteen came for just one hour and four came for two hours. I never saw the same customer twice. I don't know what I'm doing wrong. Nancy and Sandra have lots of customers who keep coming back but my customers never come back to see me.

Candy and Vicky were late but they had been to buy Thai fruit in Chinatown so Oliver didn't mind. Candy had £1,500 for Oliver and Vicky had £1,400. In all we girls gave Oliver £11,100. That is what he earns for one week. One week! In Thailand most people don't earn that much in two years!

After I gave Oliver his £1,100 share I had £2,200. Oliver said I should give him £1,600 of what I owed him and I said that was okay but I was a bit worried about how little money I had to spend. My rent costs £450 a week, though I did pay two months in advance. I still have a lot of bills to pay, though. London is so expensive. I have to pay council tax every month and then I have to pay for water and electricity and for my cable TV and Netflix. It's much more expensive than Thailand. I buy a lot of Evian water. Everyone says that it's okay to drink the tap water in London but I don't like the taste of it so I buy Evian water instead. Water is so expensive in England. In Thailand water costs a few baht for a bottle but here it costs almost a pound a bottle. Then I have to buy beer and wine and soft drinks for my customers and I am using so much shampoo and shower gel.

When I first came to London I rented a room in a house near my school in Hampstead. I paid £60 a week. But Oliver says that to work as an agency girl you have to have a nice flat so that the customer feels happy. My flat is really nice. Oliver found it for me. It's not far from Paddington Station and it's got one bedroom and a pretty sitting room with a sofa and a television and a kitchen at one end. The bathroom is very clean and there is a really powerful shower. I shower a lot. I shower when I get up, I shower before and after I go with a customer, and I shower before I go to bed.

I put candles everywhere in the flat when a customer comes around. That was Cat's idea. She said that customers like candles and she's right. I suppose it makes them feel romantic. Cat says I should always keep wine and beer and soft drinks in the fridge to give to customers and chocolates, too. I have to pay for it all, of course. It's like I have to pay for everything. I have to pay for the sexy clothes I wear and for the photographs that they put on the agency's website and for the flat. I had to pay for the candles, for all the towels that the customers use and for condoms and oil and KY Jelly. Pay, pay, pay. But at least I am getting a lot of money. I just wish I could keep more of it myself.

After we had paid Oliver, Cat brought out lots of Thai food and Thai whiskey and everyone started eating and drinking and telling stories. Then Oliver bought out a pack of cards and he played with the girls until dawn. Oliver was really lucky, I think he won almost £2,000. Nancy lost the most. I think she lost more than a thousand pounds which is crazy because she had to sleep with ten men to make a thousand pounds. I don't understand why the girls don't keep a hold of their money.

Chapter 11

Wednesday March 18. Hundreds of people in England have caught the Covid virus now. I don't understand what is happening. I think more people in England have the virus than in Thailand. Yesterday the Government here said that people should not go to pubs or theatres and that they should work from home if they can. I work from home so that is okay for me. Sometimes I go to see a client in their hotel room but usually they come to see me. I phoned my mum and she said that some people in Thailand have the virus but not many. She told me not to worry but I made her promise to take good care of Ice. I do not want my son to get sick.

Then in the evening John called me from the language school. He said the Government is forcing all schools to close from Friday. He said they are not allowed to have any more classes. Actually that is good for me because I don't really want to go to school, I want to earn money. John said they will try to open again as soon as possible and I told him not to worry. He said they would set up online lessons so that the students can continue their studies. Actually I am very happy not to be studying, I am improving my English by talking to my clients.

Chapter 12

Friday March 20. Now the Government has closed all pubs, restaurants, gyms, cinemas, nightclubs and theatres. They said that Covid is still spreading so people should stay at home. I hope people don't stay at home because if they do then I will have no customers and that will not be good for me. But I hope they do not shut the hotels. If they do that then there will be no tourists and quite a few clients are tourists or people staying in hotels on business.

I was busy this week. Two customers on Monday, one on Tuesday but he stayed three hours and two customers on Wednesday and three on Thursday. That's ten hours which means I have earned £1,000 for myself in four days. And the beginning of the week is always quieter. Friday is always the busiest day. That's what Cat says.

Most of the customers were okay but they are all starting to look the same. I can't remember what they look like five minutes after they leave.

On Tuesday Oliver phoned me to tell me that a customer called Tony had posted a review and that he said I was one of the worst girls he had ever been with, that I didn't smile and that I wasn't as pretty as the pictures on my website. I knew Tony was just angry because I insisted that he used a condom and I told that to Oliver. Oliver said that Tony was a good customer and that I should have done more to make him happy and that made me want to cry. What was I supposed to do? Let him make love to me without a condom? What if I got sick? What if I got pregnant? I'm not taking the pill any more now that I am in England. Sometimes I think that Oliver cares more about money than he does about the girls who work for him. Tony is just one customer. How much does he spend with the agency? Three hundred pounds a week? Four hundred? Even if he spent six hundred pounds a week then Oliver would only get two hundred and I give Oliver much more than that. Oliver should be sticking up for me, not telling me that I've done something wrong. It's not fair.

On Wednesday I did laundry. Lots of laundry. Every time a customer comes I have to use two towels. I spread one on the bed and I put another in the bathroom. I always give clean towels to my customers but Sandra says there is no point, all you have to do is let them dry and you can use them again. I don't think that's right. I don't like using someone else's towel so I don't see why my customers should. I hope the laundry doesn't close because of Covid. I don't know what I will do if the laundry closes.

By Monday all the white towels I had bought were dirty so I went out and bought another ten. By Wednesday I had sixteen dirty towels to wash and I had to do them in four loads because the towels are big. There is a washing machine in the flat, one of those that you load from the front. It's a dryer, too. It took about four hours to wash and dry a load so in all it took sixteen hours to do them all. I felt like a washerwoman by the time I'd finished. My mother still does all her washing by hand. Can you believe that? She uses cold water and washes everything in a big plastic bowl behind her house and then hangs them up to dry.

Kung keeps calling me and asking me for money. It's like that's all he cares about now. Before he said he loved me and that he'd leave his wife to be with me and Ice but now all that he talks about is money. At first I just said that I didn't have it and that he'd have to wait but now I just don't answer his calls. There's nothing I can do. I'm earning more money than I ever thought I'd earn but I don't get to keep any of it. It all goes to Oliver and what's left I need to buy things for the flat. I know I'm going to get a big electricity bill because I'm using the washing machine so much.

I hope I get another customer tonight. Then when it's about two o'clock in the morning I'll phone Ice and tell him how much I miss him. I love to see him and hear his voice, especially when he laughs. But I get sad when he cries and he says that he misses me. He always asks when I'll go back to see him, and I don't know how to answer that.

Chapter 13

Monday March 23. Covid is getting worse in England. Now the Government has said that all non-essential shops have to close and people have to stay at home and the police are going to make sure that people don't leave their houses. The only shops that can stay open are food shops, pharmacies, hardware shops and newsagents. And banks. That means that hotels are having to close so we won't be able to visit clients in hotels. In fact there won't be any clients in hotels. The hotels will be empty. And they are closing the churches. I don't understand. I don't think the Thai Government would ever try to close the temples. The people would not allow that.

I went to the pharmacy to see the Indian guy and he said he had sold all his masks and latex gloves. He had some hand sanitiser but it was expensive. When he had first told me I should buy it he was charging 99p but now a bottle costs £5. He said it wasn't his fault, his supplier had raised his prices. And he said I should buy toilet rolls. I laughed because I thought he was joking but he was serious. He said his supplier had said that there was going to be a shortage. I went to a supermarket and bought twelve rolls of toilet paper, just in case.

Sandra and Nancy came around to my flat on Sunday evening before we went to take our money to Oliver. They both said my flat was really nice. Sandra said I should buy a big mirror and hang it at the end of the bed. She said that men get really turned on if they can watch themselves and the more turned on they were the quicker they came. Sandra's boyfriend is an American. He works for a bank in London and he drives a Porsche. I don't understand how he can be her boyfriend when he knows what job she does. Why would a boyfriend want his girlfriend to sleep with other men? It doesn't make sense.

Nancy asked me where I hid my money and I showed her the drawer in the kitchen. I had earned £2,100 during the week and it was in envelopes in the drawer. They both laughed and said that I should be more careful. Sometimes girls were robbed, Nancy said, and I should look for hiding places. Under the carpet or in the wardrobe, somewhere where it would be hard to find. And Sandra said I shouldn't keep all my money in the same place because that way if I was robbed I could tell the robber one hiding place and he wouldn't get all my money.

We shared a taxi to Sloane Square but Nancy and Sandra got out quickly and I had to pay. It was only £7 so I didn't mind. Candy, Vicky, Alice and Wanda were already there, drinking Thai whiskey and watching a Thai soap opera on TV. Oliver and Cat came late, with a load of food that they'd brought from a Thai restaurant in Fulham. They said the restaurant wasn't serving customers any more but they did takeaway. All the staff were wearing masks and Oliver and Cat weren't allowed inside, they had to wait on the pavement.

I gave Oliver his £700 commission and another £1,000 to pay off what I owe him. That means I only owe him another £3,350 which I guess I will be able to pay off in three weeks. Then I will be able to keep all my money.

I still haven't had any customers come back and I don't understand why. I do try to be nice to them and I try to smile even when I'm tired. Alice gave Oliver £2,400. That means she earned £7,200 last week. That sounded impossible to me. The client pays £150 an hour which means she worked forty hours. I asked Sandra if that meant that Alice had sex with forty men and she laughed. Alice heard her laughing and got a bit angry because she thought we were laughing at her but I explained that I didn't understand how she could work so hard. Alice glared at me and said it wasn't any of my business.

Later, Cat took me to one side and explained that Alice had a lot of regular customers and several paid for her to sleep with them overnight. They paid £1,200 for nine hours, starting at eleven o'clock at night and finishing at eight o'clock in the morning. They paid a cheaper rate per hour but for most of the time the customer was asleep. One of Alice's regular customers, an American from New York, had booked her for four nights at his hotel. So for four nights she had earned £4,800.

I was amazed. I wish that I had a customer like that. I don't understand why Alice is so lucky. She isn't as pretty as me and she has dark skin and tattoos and she smokes and drinks and swears. I want to find out what she does to get customers who will pay so much money.

But now that hotels are closing because of Covid, that won't happen again for a while.

I was the worst-earning girl again this week. Nancy gave Oliver £1,100, Candy gave him £1,200, Sandra and Vicky both gave him £1,300. Wanda had £1,400 for him. After we had eaten the food they started to play cards. I watched. Sandra and Nancy kept asking me to join in but I said that I didn't have enough money. They laughed and said that if I was lucky then it wouldn't matter how much money I had but I didn't feel lucky so I just watched them play. Oliver was very lucky and he won a lot of money. They finished playing cards at four o'clock in the morning and I went back with Nancy to her flat. I don't like sleeping alone any more. I feel so lonely when I am in my apartment.

Chapter 14

Thursday March 27. Today Thailand has closed all its airports. No one can fly in and that means Thais and foreigners. I saw the news on Thai TV and at first I didn't understand what was happening. How can a country close all its airports? And it is not just the airports. People can not walk across the borders from Laos, Burma, Cambodia or Malaysia. It is like the country is shut. It made me feel very lonely because it means I can not fly back to Thailand, even if I wanted to. Now I am trapped here.

Yesterday almost six hundred people died of Covid in England. Six hundred! I do not understand what is happening. Thailand has the same population as England but in Thailand only fifty people have died since the virus appeared. How can six hundred people die in one day in England? I do not understand. And England is an island so it should be easy to stop the virus getting into the country. Why are so many people dying from Covid in England but not in Thailand? Maybe it is because Thailand is a hot country and the virus does not like heat.

And now the Prime Minister of England has caught the virus. He says he will still be leader of the Government so maybe it is not too serious. I don't understand how the Prime Minster can get sick? Wasn't he careful? The Government hasn't said anything about closing the airport in London. I don't understand why they don't close all the airports because that is the best way of stopping the virus getting into the country.

I keep a bottle of hand sanitiser by the door and I ask my clients to use it when they arrive. Some do and some don't. Some of them laugh and tell me that I am silly and that there is no such thing as Covid, but I think they are wrong. I think this Covid is serious. When I go to the shops to buy food and things for work, a lot of people are wearing masks and most shops only allow a few people to go in at the same time. They call that social distancing, which really just means that you keep other people away from you. Of course in my job I can not keep people away from me, that wouldn't work. So I ask them to use the hand sanitiser and to shower before they get into bed. Nancy said that we should ask our clients to wear masks, but she was only joking.

Chapter 15

Friday March 28. This week has been really quiet. It's not just me, it's all the girls. Even Alice isn't busy. Oliver says that I shouldn't worry, it's just because people are scared of the Covid. He said he doesn't understand why so many people in England are dying of Covid. Vietnam is next to China and not one person in Vietnam has died from Covid. Not one. The virus started in China which is why they sometimes call it the Chinese Virus so you would expect countries near to China to have a lot of Covid. But Thailand has only had fifty people die and that was at the start of the year. And no one has died of Covid in Vietnam. Oliver says Vietnam started testing people for Covid in January and they closed the border with China. Then in the middle of March they put anyone who entered the country into a quarantine centre for fourteen days. And anyone who was in contact with someone who had the virus was also put into quarantine. That is probably why Thailand has shut its airports, they want to be like Vietnam and not like England.

Most nights now I stay with Nancy because otherwise it's just so boring, lying on my sofa watching television and waiting for the phone to ring. At least if I stay with Nancy we can talk and eat together. She's quite funny, like a big kid. Actually, she is a kid. She's only nineteen and she's been in London for almost a year. She came on a student visa, like me, but her visa was only for six months so now she's overstaying. That's not a problem in London because no one checks. If the police catch her working as an escort then she might have a problem, but otherwise no one ever asks to see a passport or a visa. It's not like Thailand where the immigration police are always catching illegal immigrants from Burma or Vietnam and putting them in prison. Nancy comes from a poor family in Isarn and she says that she sends a lot of money home to her parents but she plays cards a lot and her flat is full of things that she's bought. Stupid things like Gucci shoes and Louis Vuitton handbags. Some of them are still in their boxes. She says that shopping makes her feel good. I think she's just a kid who doesn't know how to take care of her money. The fact that the Government has now closed most shops means she will save money, but she probably won't see it that way.

Chapter 16

Monday March 29. There was a new girl at the Sloane Square flat today. Her name is Bee and she says she's from Thailand but I think she's from Laos. She's very short and dark-skinned but quite pretty. I think she's about my age. Sandra has paid for Bee's contract. Bee is her real name, she says, but she's working under the name of Belinda. I hadn't heard about the contract system before but Nancy explained it to me when I went home with her. Some girls come to the UK the way I did. They go to the British Embassy in Bangkok and get a student visa or a tourist visa. It's not difficult so long as you own property or have money in the bank or if you have someone like Kung to sponsor you. But if you can't get a visa by the normal route, there are agencies who can do it for you. The going rate, Nancy said, is £6,000. If a girl in Bangkok has £6,000 she can buy a visa and a ticket to London. But £6,000 is a lot of money. Most people in Thailand would have to work for more than a year to earn £6,000. So if a girl doesn't have £6,000, she takes out a contract. Someone else pays the £6,000 for her and then when she gets to England she has to pay back £18,000. That's what Sandra is doing. She paid the £6,000 for Bee to get to London, now Bee has to pay back Sandra £18,000. That means that Sandra will make a profit of £12,000. I know that £18,000 is a lot of money but if Bee works really hard she might be able to pay it back in two months and she has a one-year visa so she will have plenty of time to earn money for herself. But it made me realise how lucky I am. I only have to pay back Oliver the money for my flat.

Bee started work on Tuesday but she had £700 for Oliver, the same as me. That means she had earned £2,100 and got to keep £1,400. I think she gave most of that to Sandra. Sandra has also loaned Bee the money for her flat in South Kensington, not far from her own flat. It seems like a good way of making money. I think once I've paid Oliver what I owe him that I might buy a contract and bring in a girl from

Thailand. I could save £6,000 in a month or so and if I invest that in a girl's contract then I'll make a profit of £12,000.

I paid Oliver £800 towards what I owed him, which means that now I owe him just £2,550. Two or three more weeks and hopefully I won't owe him anything.

When I got back to Nancy's flat I asked her if she liked working with other girls. She said it was easy because you only had to do half the work. Most customers come very quickly when they are with two girls and sometimes you don't even have to have sex with them. I asked her if she was shy when she saw another girl naked and she said that she was the first few times but that it's just work so it doesn't matter. It's a job and if two people do a job it's easier than when one person does a job. She said that it was great working with Candy because Candy really liked sex so she would let the customer do whatever they wanted.. That meant that when Nancy worked with Candy, Nancy had to hardly do anything at all. I asked Nancy how many of the girls she had worked with. She said she had worked with Candy and Sandra several times and with Vicky once. On the website there were photographs of her with Candy. They were lesbian pictures, kissing and holding each other. She said that most of the time in the studio she was laughing until the photographer spoke sternly to her. She said that if I wanted she would work with me and show me what it was like. I laughed but I thought that maybe I might try it. I have to do something to make more money. So far I haven't been able to send any money back to Thailand because I am giving most of my profit to Oliver and the rest of the money goes to pay my expenses.

Chapter 17

Wednesday April 1. Yesterday was a quiet day. It was raining very hard so I think customers weren't thinking about sex. Maybe they are worried about Covid and don't want to go out. They said on the TV that 3,850 people had died of the virus in England. Almost four thousand. I don't understand why so many people are dying. Nobody is dying of Covid in Thailand now. Nancy phoned me at nine o'clock and said that she had no customers so why didn't I go to her flat because she and Candy were cooking Thai food. I had some cooked prawns and some strawberries that I'd bought from the Tesco supermarket so I took them. There was a queue to get into the supermarket and there was a big man in a fluorescent jacket telling people that they had to wear a mask and stay six feet away from everyone else. They had run out of toilet rolls, but that is okay because I still have some.

Candy said she was having her period so she wasn't working. Some girls carry on working when they have their period but Candy said she got stomach cramps and sex made them worse so she always took three days off when she had her period, sometimes four. I am lucky because my period only comes for two days and it doesn't hurt much.

Candy is quite thin and tall and really the first time I saw her I thought she might be a ladyboy. Her voice is quite deep and she has a square jaw but she's definitely a girl and I think farangs find her very sexy. She has really nice eyes and long eyelashes. She cooked Pad Thai and added my prawns, and Nancy had some chicken that she fried with chillies. Candy drank whiskey with her food and Nancy had a bottle of Heineken beer.

Candy was telling us about the faces she made when she wanted to make a customer feel sexy. She showed us, it was so funny. She sort of lifts her chin and half opens her mouth and half closes her eyes. She's right, it does look really sexy. She says that she makes a sexy face and then takes off her bra slowly and that makes a customer so horny that they come really quickly. I practised in front of the mirror and she showed me how to get my mouth just right. I kept laughing but it worked, I did look really sexy.

After we had eaten our food Nancy got a pack of cards and said she wanted to play. I said I didn't want to gamble but she said we could just play for spare change. She said we could play for a pound a game. Candy wanted to play and she said that two wasn't much fun and that when three played it was a better game so I said okay, I'd try. The game was quite easy. It is called Pok Gow. Someone is the dealer, and you take turns for who is the dealer. Every player gets two cards. But if you want to play twice, you can. And there are two more cards in the middle that you can also bet on, but you have to decide if you want to bet after you have seen the first card. If you want to bet on it then you put your money in the middle.

Farangs play a game like it called Blackjack or Twenty-One but Pok Gow is more fun because there are more ways of winning. You need to get nine to win. An ace counts as one, and a king, queen and jack do not count. If someone's cards add up to eight or nine straight away, they have to show them. If their hand is better than the dealer's hand, they double their money. If the two cards are in the same suit then they get three times their money.

If no one has an eight or nine with their two cards, you can choose if you want another card or not. If you take another card, and your cards add up to more than the dealer's cards, then you win double your stake. If all the cards are the same suit, then you get three times your stake. If the cards make a run, like a six, seven and an eight, then you get three times your stake. If you have three picture cards, then you win three times your stake. If you get a run of three cards and they are in the same suit, then you win five times your stake. But if the dealer has a run of cards in the same suit then everybody loses five times their stake! It sounds complicated and it was quite difficult at first but after a while it was fun. We were all laughing a lot and sometimes it was exciting. Once I won £8 on two hands. By the end of the evening I had won more than £20. Nancy and Candy said I was lucky and that I should play with them next time we went to the flat in Sloane Square. I'm not sure if that is a good idea. When the girls play in the flat they play for £20 a game and that means if the dealer gets a good hand you can lose £100.

Chapter 18

Monday April 6. I played cards with the girl's at Oliver's flat yesterday and I won! I can't believe it. I won £800. I was so happy. I'd have to sleep with eight men to earn £800 and I got it just playing Pok Gow. Oliver said I was really lucky. He won too. Actually, he won more than me. All the girls lost money except for me. It was a bit scary at first because it was twenty pounds a hand but I started winning right from the start. Oliver was the dealer and I got nine straight away, then eight, then a got a run of hearts – the two, three and four – and I won £100. At one point I was winning more than £1,000 but then towards the end I started losing a bit. We finished playing at four o'clock in the morning. If I played cards every week and won £800 every time then it wouldn't matter so much how many customers I had.

Business was better last week. I had £950 for Oliver. Plus I gave him £1,500 towards what I owe him so now I only have to pay him £1,050. I am going to send the rest of the money I won back to Thailand. I thought Covid would mean that our clients would stay home and not go out, but most of my clients say they don't care and that sex is more important than Covid. I hope they continue to think that way.

Alice wasn't the best earning girl last week. It was Bee, the new girl. Alice had £2,100 for Oliver but Bee had £2,200. That meant she earned £6,600 in her second week. Alice didn't seem very happy, especially when Oliver started teasing her. I wanted to ask Bee how she did it, how she managed to make so much money so quickly, but I didn't want to ask her while Alice was there because Alice might get angry. She kept glaring at Bee all the time and I think she wanted to fight with her. I don't understand why she was angry because it's not as if we are in competition.

Nancy only had £1,100 for Oliver. She told me she didn't feel like working last week. She kept telling Oliver that she didn't feel well but really she met a guy in a pub in the King's Road and she wanted to see him. FFF, she said, but I didn't understand what she meant. She laughed. 'Fuck For Free,' she said. He was young and fit and she made love to him because she liked it. That didn't make any sense to me. She's like me, she's a working girl which means that we sell sex. Why would she want to have sex with someone for free ? The last thing I want right now is sex with anyone. Sex is my job, it's how I earn my money. Maybe when I have finished with this job I might start having sex for fun again, but I'm not sure if that will ever happen. Being a working girl has changed me, I know that. I used to like sex with my boyfriend, I would do whatever he wanted to make him happy, but now when I'm having sex all I think about is the money. I smile and I moan and I sweet talk but I don't mean it, I just think how much I'm earning.

Candy had £2,000 for Oliver because a regular customer had booked her for two days. Candy does domination sometimes. She wears shiny plastic outfits with high-heeled boots and says that she whips her customers but not too hard. Some of her customers don't even want to have sex with her. They want her to say bad things and to hit them but she doesn't screw them or anything. I asked Candy if anyone could do domination and she said it was difficult. You were like an actress and if you didn't play the part perfectly the customer wouldn't be happy. She said that I could do a session with her one day if I wanted. Some customers wanted to be abused by two girls. I'm not sure if I could do domination. I think I would find it too funny and I would just laugh.

Sandra had £1,600 for Oliver. I had taken my Louis Vuitton bag with me. It's a lovely bag and I always used to take it with me when I did outcall at a hotel and she said she loved it and that we should go shopping together. I think she had forgotten that almost all the shops are shut now because of Covid. I like Sandra, she's sweet and kind.

The British Prime Minister is in hospital now. He is very sick. I hope he does not die.

Chapter 19

Sunday April 12. I don't understand why men pay for sex. I know that sounds like a funny thing for an escort girl to say, because that's how I make my money, but if I was a man I don't think I would pay to have sex with a girl. It's easy for a man to come. He can do it himself with his hand. So why would he want to pay £150 or more to have a girl make him come? Some of the men who come to see me don't even talk to me. They just take off their clothes and lie down on the bed. Some of my customers don't want to have sex, they just want me to use my hand or my mouth. I suppose they think that having sex with a working girl means that they might catch something. I don't think they realise how careful I am. So what are they paying for? They're just paying to come, and I don't see why they think that it's worth £150 just to have an orgasm.

Some of my customers do want more. They want to talk to me and they like to kiss. I suppose they want to feel that they are with a girlfriend, but then if that's what they want why do they go to see a working girl? They must realise that they can't have a working girl as a girlfriend. Working girls have sex for money, they're not looking for a boyfriend or a husband. If they want a girlfriend then they should be out meeting people, not paying for sex. Some of my customers ask me for my phone number but I never give it to them. I tell them that if they want to talk to me then they have to call the agency and make an appointment.

I don't think a woman would ever pay for sex. I like sex, or at least I like sex with somebody I care for. I really enjoyed sex with Kung and I liked making love to Ice's father. But if I went for weeks or months without sex I'd rather take care of myself than pay a stranger for sex. I suppose men and women are different and that's all there is to say about it.

Chapter 20

Monday April 13. A lot of people are still dying from Covid in England. More than eight hundred every day. But no one is dying from Covid in Thailand or Vietnam. The Prime Minister didn't die. He left hospital yesterday. I don't understand how he got sick with the virus. You would think that the Government would take care of its Prime Minister. It's like everyone in England is scared of the virus but they are not protecting themselves.

Yesterday Nancy and I went to Chinatown to buy some Thai fruits to take to the flat in Sloane Square and I wanted to buy some Ma-Ma noodles. We had to queue outside and we had to wear masks. There was a Chinese girl wearing a facemask with a sort of gun that she used to take the temperature of everyone who went inside. While we were queuing two farangs started shouting at the people working in the supermarket. They said the Chinese were dirty and that it was their fault that Covid was in England. They were telling the Chinese that they should go home and that British people shouldn't be buying Chinese food because Chinese food will give you Covid. I don't think they were drunk, I think they were just mean. They weren't wearing masks, either. They were getting close to the people in the queue and shouting at them so they should have been wearing masks.

After a few minutes of them shouting half a dozen Chinese men arrived and I thought there was going to be a fight like in a Bruce Lee movie but the farangs went away.

When we got to the flat in Sloane Square we gave the fruit to Cat and then gave our money to Oliver. It was my best week ever, because I had done three outcall jobs and two of them had been for three hours. In all I had earned £4,200 so I had £1,400 for Oliver and I was able to pay off the rest of the money I owed him. It meant that from now one, everything I earned, except for the agency's commission, was mine to keep. I was so happy that I couldn't stop smiling.

Alice had £1,900 for Oliver and Bee had £1,800. I could see that Alice was really happy that she was top girl again, and she kept smiling at Bee but I could see that she was only smiling with her mouth, not her eyes. Sandra had £1,500 for Oliver and Candy had £1,600. Nancy had the same as me. Wanda had £1,200 and Vicky had £1,000 for him. That meant in all we gave Oliver almost £12,000. He had it all piled up on his coffee table. If he earned that every week he would get more than half a million pounds a year, can you believe it! Maybe I should start my own agency. I don't think it's very difficult. You just need a website and then all you do is answer the phone and arrange a meeting. I think I would rather run an agency than sleep with men for money. Even though more people are dying of Covid, most of my clients don't believe in it. They think the Government is making Covid sound worse than it really is.

After we had eaten our Thai food we sang karaoke for a couple of hours, and then Oliver said he wanted to play cards so we played Pok Gow. I won again, but this time I only won £200. Bee won too. She played really well and at one point she was up £4,000 but then she got a bit drunk and lost half of that. She still made a profit of £2,000, though. Oliver won the most. Oliver drinks beer while we play but I noticed that he doesn't drink a lot. The girls do, though. Not me, because I don't like alcohol, but the rest of the girls drink beer or Thai whiskey and Cat is always pouring more into their glasses as if she wants them drunk. We didn't finish until four o'clock in the morning and I went home to sleep with Nancy. She was very drunk and spent an hour in the bathroom, throwing up. I felt a bit sorry for her, but it was her own fault.

Chapter 21

Thursday April 16. Yesterday I was really busy. I had three bookings, all incall. Two were for one hour and one was for an hour and a half. I was really tired so at midnight I sent Oliver a text message saying that I didn't want to work any more that day. I phoned Nancy and asked her if I could go around and see her. She said that was okay and that she was cooking Thai food so I went to the supermarket and bought some fruit including a big watermelon. I looked for toilet rolls but they didn't have anyway. And there was no rice. I don't understand why farangs have been buying up all the rice. There as no pasta, either. But we both love eating watermelon, so it was okay. We cut it in half with a big knife and then eat half each with a spoon. Lovely. Or as we say in Thai, arroy mak!

While we were eating, one of Nancy's mobile phones beeped. It was a text message. She looked at it and laughed and then showed it to me. It was one of her customers, telling her that he missed her. She sent him a message back saying that she missed him. She called him darling. I was really surprised because I never give my number to customers but Nancy says she does it all the time. She said it meant nothing because she was using a Pay-As-You-Go T-Mobile SIM card so she could throw it away whenever she wanted and the customers only know her as Nancy so they don't even know her real name. She said that every night she sends the same message to ten of her customers, saying that she misses them and she hopes to see them again. She sends them all the same message! And they all believe it. She says that it's like advertising. When they get the message they think about her and hopefully they'll feel horny. If they feel horny, they'll want to see her. I asked her if she saw them on her own but she said no, she always told them to phone the agency and make an appointment. She said that Oliver would be really angry if he found out that a girl was seeing a customer privately. I can understand why. It's only fair that he gets his share because he does own the agency and he does get us all our customers. If it wasn't for Oliver, we wouldn't have any customers at all.

Nancy phones some of her customers for phone sex. She talks to them while they play with themselves and make themselves come. She says she likes doing it and sometimes she plays with herself while she's doing it. She's a bit crazy and I think she really likes sex. I like sex, too, but sex with customers is different from having sex with a husband or a boyfriend. Sex with customers is all about money, nothing else. But I think I might start giving my phone number to some of my customers. The nice ones, anyway.

Chapter 22

Saturday April 18. Kung keeps phoning me and asking for money to pay the builders and to pay the bank. I think he thinks that now I'm in London I'm rich. He keeps telling me that he loves me and that he misses me but when I ask when he'll leave his wife he says that he can't. I told him I don't want to be his Mia Noi, his second wife. I want us to live together as a family. I told him that I'm not scared of his wife, but he must divorce her. I wish I'd never started building the house. It was supposed to be our home together and now it's just a reminder that we aren't together. It is a nice house, though. I designed it with an architect and spent ages choosing the fittings for the bathroom and the kitchen. I'm going to have a spa bath and a huge shower and a huge television in the sitting room but none of it will mean anything if I don't have a husband.

I sent Kung £1000 yesterday. He said he needed it urgently so I did it by Western Union. There are lots of places that do Western Union transfers close to Paddington Station. You give them the cash in pound notes and they tap the details into their computer. You give them the name of the person who is to get the money and the country they are in, and they give you a password. You give your friend the password and then they go to any Western Union office and show their ID and give the password and they get the money. It costs about £50 to send £1000 which I think is quite cheap because they do it really quickly. I asked Kung if he'd use some of the money to buy Ice a present. He loves Mickey Mouse so I asked Kung to buy him something with Mickey Mouse on it.

I'm going to send my mum some money but I don't want to use Western Union because I don't want her walking around with a lot of cash. I will probably post it to her. It's great to be able to send my family money. Now that I've paid Oliver what I owe him I'm starting to earn real money. So far this week I've earned more than £3,000, £2000 for me and £1000 for Oliver.

I've also been to a customer's house. He was a nice man, called Robert, and he had a house in South Kensington. It was a big house with lots of bedrooms but he said that he lived there alone. He told Oliver he wanted me to wear a school uniform so I had it on under my Kenzo coat. As soon as I took my coat off he knelt down and started kissing my feet. That's all he wanted to do for two hours, to kiss and lick my feet while he played with himself. He paid me £420 and gave me £50 for my taxi. Men are so funny. He was obviously really rich and he was quite good looking. Tall and a bit skinny but with a kind face. Why would he want to kiss a girl's feet? I found it a bit ticklish, but it was an easy way to make money. When he'd finished he asked me if I'd give him my phone number so I did. He's the first customer I've given my number to. I wonder if he'll call me, and if he does I wonder what I'll say to him.

Chapter 23

Monday April 20. It worked! Robert sent me a text message saying that he missed me and I sent him one back that said 'I miss you too, honey.' Then about an hour after I sent the text message Oliver phoned me to say that Robert had booked me again for Sunday afternoon and that this time he wanted to see me for four hours! Four hours outcall costs the customer £690. Almost £700 and he doesn't even want to have sex with me! He wanted me to wear the school uniform again and I did, though this time I went out to Marks and Spencer and bought some knee-length white socks, the sort that school kids wear. I had to queue for half an hour to get into the store and when I was in I had to follow arrows on the floor to show which direction to walk.

Robert loved the socks. This time he made a snack for me, peanut butter sandwiches and a glass of milk, and he sat in the kitchen and watched me eat it. I wasn't really hungry but I ate the sandwiches and drank the milk because I could see that it made him happy. We went to his bedroom and this time he asked me to take off my top and my bra but he didn't want me to take my panties off. He kissed me up and down my legs and then slid off the socks and spent an hour just licking my feet. When his time was up he gave me the £690 plus a £50 tip. He kissed me on top of the head and said that next time I saw him he wanted me to call him 'Daddy' which I thought was a bit strange but he is the customer so I'll do whatever he wants to make him happy.

I went to the Sloane Square flat with Nancy. We went in an Uber because there are almost no taxis driving around the streets. When you use an Uber the driver wears a mask and you have to wear a mask as well. And they always have sanitiser in the car. I told Nancy about Robert and she said that I should tell him that she was my young sister and that we could both go and see him. I said I'd ask him but I don't think I will because I want to keep Robert as my own customer. I think Nancy would want to have sex with Robert and that's not what he wants.

I had £1,600 to give Oliver. It was my best week ever. I had earned £4,800 during the week, and £1,110 was from Robert. I am starting to understand how valuable regular customers are and why it is important to be nice to them. Robert had paid me £1,110 and I hadn't even had to have sex with him. I would have to have sex with seven customers for one hour each to get the same money. At just before midnight I went to the bathroom and sent Robert a text message. 'I miss you, Daddy' is what I sent. I was sure that it would make him horny and sure enough, ten minutes later I got a text back from him. 'I miss you too, baby. See you again soon.' I hope he does book me again. It was easy money.

Nancy had just £900 because she had been spending time with her kik. Kik is what we call a boyfriend, sort of, more like someone we have sex with for fun. Nancy has sex with the boy for free. FFF, she says. He's nineteen like her and she showed me a picture on her phone. He is quite handsome, but I don't understand why she gives away what we are supposed to be selling.

Everyone was earning good money. If anything Covid is good for business because men get bored staying at home and they can't go to pubs or bars so then they decide that seeing an escort is the best thing to do.

We ate Thai food and sang some karaoke and then we played cards. I wasn't so lucky and lost £600.

Chapter 24

Saturday April 25. Yesterday was a busy day. Oliver phoned me at two o'clock in the afternoon and told me that I had a booking for three o'clock and that the customer's name was John and that he wanted me to wear school uniform. John said that he was a teacher and he wanted me to call him Sir while he made love to me. It was funny because I kept thinking about John at my language school and that made me want to laugh. John wasn't a very nice man and he was a bit rough with me. I think he enjoyed hurting me.

Then Oliver phoned me again at five o'clock to tell me that I had a two-hour booking for five-thirty. His name was Gordon. Gordon was nice. He was about forty and a bit fat but he had a nice smile and he kept saying how pretty I was. Gordon made me laugh, too. He kissed me when he went and said that he'd see me again and that made me happy. I gave him my phone number and said that he could call me if he wanted and he seemed really pleased. He paid me £300 for the two hours and afterwards he gave me a fifty pound tip.

We always have to ask for the money before we do anything. I feel a bit shy doing that but Oliver says that if we don't the customer might try to get sex for free. They will have sex and then say that they haven't got any money and that they have to go to the ATM and then you never see them again. That happened to Nancy once. A customer stayed for four hours and he was so nice looking that she didn't ask him for the money. He had sex with her lots of times and he drank a whole bottle of wine while he was there. Then he said that he didn't have enough money but that he'd get some from the bank. She never saw him again. She told Oliver and he said that she still had to pay him his commission even though she hadn't been paid and that didn't seem fair to me.

Not long after Gordon had left Oliver phoned me again and said that I had a booking for three hours. I was really happy because that meant I would be working for six hours in the day but only with three customers. His name was Richard and he paid me straight away and he asked me if I'd give him a bubble bath. I hadn't done that before and I didn't have any bubble stuff but I said I would have a bath with him. I cleaned him and then started to massage him between the legs and then he said he wanted to make love so we had sex in the bath with me on top. It was funny because water started to go everywhere. He came really quickly but his dick stayed hard. Really hard. I dried him with a towel and then we went to the bedroom and he made love to me again, this time doggy-style which I don't really like because it goes in really deep and hurts a bit. It took him longer to come this time, but he was still hard. I gave him a massage and then he wanted to make love again, this time on top of me. He put my legs over his shoulders and he was so deep that there were tears in my eyes. He wasn't rough, though, not like the teacher had been, but he was quite big and he pushed really deep inside me.

When he'd finished I thought that would be it. Most men can come twice, especially if I am really sexy with them, but not many can manage three times. But Richard was still hard and after five minutes he was doing it again, this time with me on top. He made me make love to him for almost half an hour and I was exhausted, and then finally he came. Then he said he wanted another bath and I thought that meant he wanted to shower and then go home, but no, he wanted me in the bath with him and he made love to me again.

In all he made love to me eight times in three hours and he was as hard at the end as he was at the start. I could barely walk and I was so sore. After he had gone I phoned Oliver and said that I couldn't see any more customers. I told him that Richard had had sex with me eight times and Oliver laughed. He said that he had probably been taking Viagra. I thought Oliver was joking. Why would a customer take Viagra before going to see a working girl? Our job is to make them feel good and to have sex with them, why would they need to take a pill? Oliver said some customers wanted to get value for money so they took Viagra before going to see the girl. That way they could have sex lots of times.

That didn't seem fair to me. It's like cheating. He paid me for three hours but he had sex eight times. He paid me £450 for the three hours so that works out at just £65 for sex. That's too cheap. I wouldn't have sex with a man for £65, not when I have to give one third of what I earn to the agency. It means he paid me just £40 each time we had sex.

Oliver said that Viagra can make men go red in the face and it makes them sniff as if they have a cold, so the next time a customer comes with a red face and a sniff I'll ask them if they have taken Viagra and if they have then I won't see them. Or I'll ask them to pay more money.

Chapter 25

Wednesday April 29. Cat took me to get some more photographs taken yesterday. She said that my pictures on the website weren't sexy enough. I thought that Covid meant that his shop would have to shut but she said it wasn't a problem. The photographer's studio is in West Kensington. He had a sign up on his door saying that he was closed because of Covid but Cat rang the bell and the photographer unlocked it for us. He's a nice man called Thomas and I think he might be gay. Cat had two dresses for me. At first I laughed when I saw them. One was a shiny black rubber dress that covered my breasts but hardly covered my backside. The other was a red vinyl dress that was also short but which had holes cut out for my breasts. Can you believe that? When I put it on, my breasts were sticking out! I thought it looked silly but Cat said it was very sexy. When I saw the photographs I realised that she was right. The idea is to get customers to come to see me so the more sexy the pictures are, the more they will want to have sex with me. I just hope that nobody in Thailand ever sees the pictures. If Kung saw them I would die of embarrassment. Cat said I should buy the dresses and she sold them to me for £300. She said that customers would see the dresses on the website and ask that I wear them when they came to see me. It makes it sexier for them, she said. The new pictures should be on the website by the end of the week.

I had three customers yesterday. The first one came at three o'clock. His name was Simon and he was about thirty five and wore a really nice suit. He was quite handsome but he had the smallest dick I had ever seen. It couldn't have been more than two inches long. It got hard and he came okay but it was so small that I could hardly feel it and I kept worrying that the condom would come off. I didn't mention how small he was and neither did he but I think we were both thinking about it. I felt sorry for him. I mean, if a girl has small breasts she can get implants, but there's nothing a guy can do about a small dick. I asked him if he would give me his phone number because I liked him and he was so pleased. I'm glad I made him happy. Before I went to sleep I sent him a text saying that I missed him, but he didn't reply.

The second customer came for two hours. I gave him champagne and kissed him and then took him into the bathroom so that we could have a bath together. I bought some bubble bath and now I ask all my customers if they want to have a bath with me because that way I am sure they are clean but it's also really easy to make them come in the bath, just using your hands. You pour shower gel over them and massage them and squeeze and they come. Then I tell them I'll give them a massage in the bedroom and often that's all they want. Or maybe oral sex. Easy money! Anyway, this customer was called Sean and he wasn't too tall, just a bit fat, but when he took off his clothes he had the biggest dick I had ever seen in my life. I am serious. I went from Simon with two inches to Sean who was at least a foot-long. I'm glad all my customers aren't as big as Sean, that's for sure. I wouldn't be able to walk.

The third customer came just after midnight. His name was Matt and he had his name tattooed in Thai on his arm, plus a tattoo of a Buddha's head. I think it is wrong to have a Buddha tattoo, it is not supposed to be a decoration. I didn't like Matt. He kept trying to speak to me in Thai but I pretended not to understand. I told him I was from Malaysia. He said he had been to Thailand many times and that he loved Thai girls but I think he just liked sex. He was a bit ugly and fat so I don't think he would find it easy to get a girlfriend in London. He had no class and he swore a lot. He said he had been to Thailand many times but the only place he had been to was Pattaya. Pattaya has a lot of prostitutes and farangs go there for sex. Matt said he liked Pattaya because in Pattaya he could have sex for just £10. He stayed for one hour and didn't give me a tip. He asked me for my phone number and said that he would take me out for a Thai meal once the restaurants are open again but I said I wasn't allowed to give a customer my number but the real reason was that I didn't want to see him again. He made me feel like a prostitute, and I don't like that. I'm not a prostitute selling sex for £10 in Pattaya. I am an escort and yes I sell my body but it's not the same.

Chapter 26

Thursday April 30. I went to see Robert yesterday. He booked me for four hours again. He always does the same thing. He gives me peanut butter sandwiches and a glass of milk and then kisses and licks my feet. It's so strange. Really, I would like to do more for him. I would like to make him happy because he is such a nice man. He is fifty years old and he has never had a wife. He lived with his mother but she died three years ago. She was very rich and she left him all her money. The house is huge. It has six bedrooms and a big garden and is full of really nice furniture and paintings. He lives there all alone. He has two maids who come in and clean the house and he can't really cook so he phones restaurants and they bring food to him. He has had girlfriends, he said, but he has never met a woman he wants to marry. He says he doesn't really want a wife but he wants a daughter. Yesterday I said he could make love to me if he wanted to but he said he didn't. He makes himself come while he kisses my feet. He said he uses Asian girls from lots of agencies but he likes me the best. I said I liked him too and that he was my favourite customer which made him smile. He has a job working for a bank, but he says that he doesn't work for the money because he has enough of that. His mother owned a jewellery store somewhere and he was her only child. Actually I think she owned quite a few jewellery stores.

He is very clever. He went to Eton which is a famous school where the Royal Family sends its sons and then he went to Cambridge which is one of the best universities in England. He makes me laugh and he seems very kind. I think he would make a very good husband for some girl. I asked him if he wanted a wife because I have friends in Udon Thani who would make really good wives but he said he was happy being single. A lot of girls in Udon Thani have married farangs but they are not as nice as Robert or as rich. Most girls in Udon Thani seem to marry old and fat farangs with very little money. I don't think the girls marry for love, I think they marry because they want a farang husband to take care of them and their families. But if they want someone to take care of them, why marry a farang who is poor? Why don't they look for a rich farang? I think the farangs who live in Udon Thani live there because it's cheap. That means they have little money. I don't think I would marry a farang with little money. I might marry a farang with a lot of money if he could take care of me, but if I did marry a farang I think I would live in his country. I have a friend called Poy who lives in Udon Thani. She is a school teacher and she has long hair and is quite pretty. She is thirty and has never married and she would be perfect for Robert. Poy can cook and she is very kind and I know she would take very good care of him. I think I will phone Poy and ask her to send me a photograph of herself and I will show it to him.

Before I came to London I never thought of marrying a farang. I always thought I would marry a Thai. Really, I thought Kung would divorce his wife and marry me but even if that didn't happen I thought I would marry another Thai man. But now I think that I could marry a farang. If I met the right one. I don't think I could marry a farang just for money, though. I think I would have to love him first. And he would have to love me and my son.

Before I went to sleep I got a text message from Simon, wishing me a good night. I sent him a message saying that I missed him and then I sent a text message to Robert, to say that I hoped I would dream about him. I called him 'Daddy' because I know that he likes that. Just before I fell asleep I got a message from Gordon saying that he missed me. I couldn't remember who Gordon was but I sent him a text message back saying that I missed him and hoped to see him soon.

Chapter 27

Saturday May 2. John called me yesterday to say that the school had put lots of lessons online which I could see whenever I want, and they would be doing live lessons through Zoom. I remembered that one of my clients had said I should buy shares in the Zoom company because more people would be talking online because of Covid. He was a smart man. I told John that I wasn't feeling well but that I would start to study online. He said he could come around with some medicine and some food for me but I told him that a girlfriend was taking care of me. I said I would try to go online next week. I really will try but I am so busy now. I usually see two or three customers a day and sometimes as many as five or six. John says that if I keep missing lessons I will never learn, but actually my English is already very good because I am talking to my clients all the time.

I studied at Ramkhamhaeng University, which is quite famous in Thailand. If I tell you how many students are at the university you will be shocked. Half a million! Really. That is how many students go to Ramkhamhaeng. It is what is called an open university and anyone can go if they want to. Actually, I found out that Vicky also went to Ramkhamhaeng University. She studied Mass Communication but she did not finish her degree. She studied for six years, she said, but she was lazy. I studied for four years and got my Bachelor of Business Administration and I was studying for my Master of Business Administration when Kung's wife found out that I was his Mia Noi and I had to leave Thailand.

Ramkhamhaeng is named after a famous king who created the Thai alphabet. The main university is in Bangkok but I studied in Udon Thani. You can study all over the country but the teachers are in Bangkok. Vicky studied near her home in Buri Ram. You go to your local campus to study and see your teachers live on a satellite link. Then on Saturdays and Sundays sometimes the teachers come to where you are so you can see them face to face.

A lot of students at Ramkhamhaeng are lazy and do not study. Most of my classmates never did any homework and were always asking me for advice on their work. I studied very hard because I thought if I had a degree and a masters then I could get a good job. I didn't know that I would be doing this job, that's for sure! An escort does not need a degree or a masters, she just needs to be pretty and give a GFE. Cat taught me about that. GFE is Girl Friend Experience. It's where the client thinks he has a girlfriend and not an escort.

I studied for my degree but I also went to a language school in Udon Thani to learn English. I knew that it was important to be able to speak English and to read and write it really well. English is the most important language in the world, I think. Maybe one day Chinese will be more important, but not now. A lot of my friends can speak English quite well because speaking English is not too difficult. In fact I think it is easier to speak English than to speak Thai. Sandra speaks really good English and she says she learned it from her customers. And Nancy knows lots of slang and swear words. She keeps saying 'innit?' which sort of means 'isn't it?' or '*chai mai*?' in Thai. But Sandra and Nancy can hardly write English at all. I studied English every day and I watched American movies. I always put the subtitles on when I watch Netflix movies so I can see and hear the words. Also I kept a diary in English. I started when I was eighteen and every day I would write what I did in English. It was very hard at first but I got better and better and now I think I write English very well. It is like most things. If you want to do them well you have to work hard at it. It is the same with my job now. If I want to do it well and earn a lot of money then I have to try hard. I do not really like being an escort but now that I am doing it I want to do it well.

Chapter 28

Sunday May 3. I have been an escort for two months. I can hardly believe it. Two months. When I first started doing this job I cried a lot but now I hardly cry at all. Sometimes I cry if a customer is not nice to me and I cry when I miss my son, but I don't cry all the time like I used to. Sometimes I even enjoy the job. Some of my customers are quite young and handsome and are good at sex, and some of them make me laugh and some tell me things I didn't know. I always ask them about their jobs and if there's something I don't understand about England they can explain things for me.

You know, I can't remember all the customers that I have seen over the past two months, even though I have all their names. It was Cat who showed me how to keep a book of my customers. I have a book with Mickey Mouse on the cover because my son Ice loves Mickey Mouse and it always makes me smile when I look at it. I keep the book in the kitchen drawer where I keep my knives and forks and spoons. That was where I used to keep my money but now I hide my money somewhere else in my room. I don't tell anyone where I hide my money.

The book is very important. All the girls at the agency have to keep a book and we take the books with us to the Sloane Square flat when we go to see Oliver and Cat on Sunday night. Cat showed me how to divide the pages up into eight columns. In the first column you put the date. In the second column you put the name of the customer. Then you put the time you met the customer and the time he left. Or the time you left if it was an outcall job. Then you put how many hours you spent with the customer. Then there's a column where you write 'I' for incall or 'O' for outcall. Then you write down how much he paid you. Then in the last column you write down how much commission you have to pay Oliver. At the end of every week you draw a line across the page and add up how much commission Oliver is to get.

So far I have paid Oliver a bit more than £9,000. Do you know how many customers I have had? I couldn't believe it when I added them up. One hundred and twelve. Before I came to England I had made love to a boy at school when I was eighteen, then Ice's father, and then Kung. Three men. That was all. And when I was working at the Thai restaurant in Camden I never had a boyfriend, even though a lot of the customers would ask me out. I was a good girl.

I didn't have sex with all one hundred and twelve men, of course. Some didn't want sex. Some wanted just oral or a massage and of course there is Robert who just likes to kiss my feet. But most of the men want to have sex so I think I have almost certainly had sex with more than eighty men. Maybe ninety. I wonder what it would look like if they were all standing together in one room. I think we would need a very big room!

Simon came to see me last night. He booked me for two hours and he brought a pizza and some DVDs with him. The first time he came to see me I had told him that I liked action movies so he bought Die Hard 3 and Déjà Vu. I had seen Die Hard 3 but I hadn't seen Déjà Vu so we watched it and ate pizza and I opened a bottle of wine. We sat on the sofa and he put his arm around me which was nice. When the movie had finished he wanted to go into the bedroom but I said that we didn't have time because his two hours was almost up. He looked a bit sad and said that he wanted to make love to me and I said that I wanted to make love to him too but that if we did he would have to book more time with the agency. I could see he wasn't happy so I kissed him and said that he had to understand me. I was a working girl and so if he wanted more than two hours he would have to speak to the agency. I kissed him again and rubbed myself against him and he laughed and said okay. He phoned Oliver and booked me for another hour and Oliver gave him a discount because it was his third hour so he only had to pay another £120. I gave him a massage and then gave him oral. He came really quickly so we didn't get to make love. I feel a bit sorry for Simon because he has such a small dick. I think it must be really difficult for him to get a girlfriend. I know some people say that the size of a man's dick isn't important and in a way that is true. It's not important unless it's really, really small, and Simon's is really, really small. But he is a nice man. He let me keep the DVDs because he said he'd bought them for me. Just before I went to sleep I got a text message from him saying that he missed me and that he wanted me to have sweet dreams. I sent him a message saying 'good night, darling' and sent it to six other customers, too. Then I sent a good night message to Robert, but I called him Daddy. He's the only customer that I call Daddy. Robert sent me a message back saying that he missed me and that he'd see me soon. Robert is the perfect customer. I am so lucky to have him.

Chapter 29

Monday May 4. Last night something terrible happened. Really terrible. It was the worst thing that has happened to me since I came to England. There was a fight between Alice and Bee and now Bee is hurt and Oliver is mad at everyone. I was so scared that I was shaking because I have never seen people fighting like that. Not girls, anyway. I went to a Muay Thai boxing match with Kung once in Udon Thani but I have never seen girls fighting before.

We had all gone to the Sloane Square flat and were showing Oliver our books and giving him our money. Cat was cooking Thai food in the kitchen and I had brought a huge watermelon, one of the biggest I had ever seen. I was cutting the watermelon into slices when Bee arrived.

Bee was grinning and she took her money out of an envelope and waved it around before giving it to Oliver. She gave him £2,800. We were all very surprised. That meant that she had earned £8,400 in one week. I asked her how she had earned so much and she said that a customer had booked her for three days. Not three overnights but for three full days and three nights. Oliver had charged him £2,100 for each day which meant that the customer had paid her £6,300. I couldn't believe it. Why would a man pay a girl £6,300 to be with him for three days? Bee said he was really rich. He worked for a big bank in New York and he earned millions of dollars a year. He had seen Bee last week and liked her so much that he had come back to see her especially. He had flown first class and was staying at a rented house in Mayfair but he spent most of his time with her in her flat in Paddington. He had brought her some gifts from America - two Chanel bags and a Rolex watch. She showed everybody her watch. It was gold and studded with small diamonds. I was so jealous. I would love to have a customer like that.

I could see that Alice wasn't happy. She kept glaring at Bee like she was angry with her, but she didn't say anything. Everybody was asking questions about Bee's customer because I think they wanted him to be their customer, too. Bee was laughing and saying that he was old and bald and fat and had five children and that she was younger than all his children. I don't know why old men want to be with young girls so much. I would think that being with a young girl would just make them feel old. Maybe it doesn't. Maybe having sex with a young girl makes them feel young again.

We ate the food that Cat had cooked and everybody said how tasty my watermelon was. Then after we had eaten the food we started to play cards. That was when the trouble started. We were playing Pok Gow as always and we were taking it in turns to deal. When it was Alice's turn to be the dealer, she gave everybody two cards. Then she gave Bee a third card. Bee picked it up but said that she didn't want it. Alice said that she had touched it so she had to have it but Bee said she didn't want it. She turned over her cards to show that she had the king and seven of hearts and she said that there's no way that she would have wanted a third card. Then Alice said that Bee was cheating and Bee said that a dog could go and fuck her mother and then Alice threw the pack of cards at Bee and screamed that she was a whore which was pretty funny actually because really we are all whores.

Bee was drinking whiskey and coke and she picked up her glass and threw it over Alice. Alice picked up the bottle of beer that Oliver had been drinking and hit Bee across the face with it. The bottle broke and there was blood everywhere. They were both screaming and Bee grabbed Alice's hair and pulled out a big chunk of it. Nancy was crying and Sandra was yelling at Alice and trying to pull her away from Bee. Oliver stood up and forced himself between the two of them and shouted at them. It was the first time I had ever seen Oliver angry.

He told Alice to go into one of the bedrooms. She was very angry and shouted at him that it wasn't fair, that he was sending all the best customers to Bee but Oliver said he wasn't going to argue with her and the she had to go to the room. Alice did as she was told.

Cat got a wet cloth from the kitchen and cleaned the cut on Bee's forehead. It was next to her eye and it wasn't too bad a cut but her eye is going to be really bruised. She was still angry and wanted to fight Alice but Oliver told her that it was over and that there was to be no more fighting. He was very angry. He said that Bee wouldn't be able to work until the bruises had gone and the cut had healed. That got

Sandra angry because she is the one who paid for Bee's contract. She said that Bee had to work because she had to pay back the money she owed Sandra. Oliver said that she couldn't work because a customer might think that Oliver had hit Bee and report him to the police. The police didn't worry about girls working but they did care when they got hurt. That got Sandra angry so she took off her shoe and tried to get into the room where Alice was to hit her but Cat stopped her. Then Sandra tried to hit Cat but Vicky and Wanda pulled her away and took the shoe off her.

Oliver said that Sandra had to take Bee home. When they had gone, Oliver went into the bedroom to talk to Alice. We couldn't hear what he said to her but he was in there for half an hour and then she came out and she was crying and she went home.

The rest of us played cards but we were all very quiet and all a bit shocked by what had happened. Oliver said that we weren't to worry, that it would be all right.

I don't know why they were fighting. We are all working girls, we should be a team, we should be helping each other not fighting each other. We finished playing cards quite early and I went home with Nancy and stayed with her. I was just about to go to sleep when her doorbell rang. It was her boyfriend. Her kik. His name is Chris and he is nineteen and quite good looking. I didn't want to stay there while he was there so I went home. Kung kept phoning me but I didn't answer the phone. I set it to silent so that I could sleep.

Chapter 30

Tuesday May 5. I watched the news on television. England now has the highest Covid death toll in Europe, the second highest in the world. More than a thousand people a day are dying of the virus. Every day. I don't understand what is happening. In Thailand nobody is dying of the virus and the Chinese say no one is dying in China. All the pubs and bars and restaurants are shut now and the only shops that are open are the food shops and the supermarkets and the pharmacies.

Kung phoned me twenty times yesterday. He knows that I can see his number when he has phoned so it's just stupid to call me so much. And what did he want to talk about? Money. He needs more money to pay the bank and to pay the builders. They are doing the kitchen now and it will cost more than 700,000 baht in total, which is more than £17,000. When I first came to England I missed Kung a lot and I was always happy to talk to him but now I think he doesn't care about me, he just cares about money. I sent him £1,000 by Western Union this week and £1,200 last week and he is still asking for more. He never asks how I am or tells me that I miss him and when I ask him when he will leave his wife he says that he doesn't want to talk about that until the house is finished. He doesn't even ask why I have so much money now. He thinks I am working in a restaurant but he must realise that I can't be earning so much by serving food. I don't think he cares what I am doing, he just wants my money. Before we used to share the cost of the house but now I think I am paying for everything.

I answered the phone when I woke up and all he said was 'call me back'. I did call him back but I don't think that's fair. If he wants to talk to me he should pay for the call. Then all he did was ask for more money. I really don't think he loves me any more but I'm not sure what I can do. I have so much of my money in the house we are building and he did all the paperwork so I am not sure what he will do if I say that I want to split up with him. Maybe he will try to keep the house. I think when we have finished the house will be worth about

2,500,000 baht which is about £65,000. Maybe if I tell him I will give him £20,000 he will let me have the house for myself. I am scared to ask him in case he says no and steals the house from me, so I just keep sending him money.

I had four customers yesterday. They were all new customers and they all stayed for one hour each. All four of them asked me for my phone number, can you believe that! Two of them were quite nice and I gave them my phone number but I didn't like the other two so much so I said no, that my agency wouldn't allow ti.

Both of them sent me text messages after they had gone, telling me how happy they were to have met me. It was funny because they used almost exactly the same words. One said 'I had such a great time with you, you made me so happy, Tom' and the other said 'It was great meeting you, now I am so happy, Dave'. I sent them both the same message. 'Thanks, honey. I hope to see you again soon'. Last thing at night I sent messages to ten customers. 'Good night, baby. I miss you.' When I woke up, eight of them had sent me messages back.

Chapter 31

Wednesday May 6. Sandra phoned me yesterday morning and asked me if I'd go with her to see Bee. I said okay and she came around to my flat and then we went to buy some fruit and chocolates and then we went to Bee's flat which is in Paddington, close to Edgware Road. Actually it is not far from Nancy's apartment but it is much nicer. It is a two bedroom flat in a new block and all the furniture was new and it had a big television. I think Bee must be paying a lot in rent.

Bee's eye looked really bad. The skin was almost green and she had a plaster over the cut. She was happy so see us but she said that she hated Alice and that if she ever saw her again she would kill her. Sandra asked her when she was going to start working again and Bee said she didn't know but Oliver had said that she couldn't work until her eye looked okay. She went into her bedroom and came out with an envelope full of money which she gave to Sandra. Sandra counted it. There was £3,000. Bee said she would give Sandra more money when she was working again.

Bee kept saying bad things about Alice but I just smiled and nodded because I didn't want to get involved. I have no problem with Bee but I have no problem with Alice, either. Then Bee said that she might stop working for the agency and that surprised me. I said that I didn't think that Oliver would be happy if she went to another agency but she said she didn't mean that, she meant she would start working on her own. Sandra said working on your own was stupid because then you had no one to take care of you but Bee laughed and pointed at her black eye and said that Oliver couldn't even protect her from one of his own girls. She said it was easy to work for yourself. All you needed was a website, and that only cost a few hundred pounds. On the website you had sexy photographs and your phone number and then customers called you instead of calling an agency. That meant that you got to keep all the money that the customer gave you.

I could see that Sandra was getting worried. I think she was scared that Bee might run away and she wouldn't get her money back. Sandra kept saying that it was better to work for an agency but I think that Bee had a point, especially if she had a customer like the American banker who bought her the Rolex watch. If you had three or four customers like him you would hardly have to work to get really big money.

Anyway, we ate some fruit and Bee made some Chinese tea and then we sang some karaoke songs. I asked her about her family and she said that her mother and father lived near Udon Thani but I don't think she is telling the truth. I think she is from Laos, but I don't know why she is lying. Maybe she is ashamed that she comes from Laos.

I asked her about the American banker and why he gave her so much money. She laughed and said it was because she had made him fall in love with her. I didn't understand. I thought that maybe she was talking about the GFE but it was more than that. She said that she had gone to an old lady who lived near her village, a sort of medicine woman who could heal people and tell fortunes. Bee said she had paid the old woman five hundred dollars for a magic potion. I thought she meant five hundred baht but no, she really did mean five hundred dollars. The potion was in a small perfume bottle. She showed it to us. It was black glass with a metal stopper. And on it was tiny writing which I think was Khmer. Actually the bottle was quite beautiful. Bee said that if you put a small drop of the perfume on your skin and then let a man smell it within three minutes, then he would fall in love with you. Well, not love exactly, but whenever he thought of you from then on for the rest of his life he would want to have sex with you. It didn't matter if he was married or if he loved someone else, he would always, always, want to have sex with you. Bee said that whenever she met a rich customer she used the perfume and every time she had used it the man had come back to see her. She showed us her mobile phone. There were lots of messages from America, from the banker, saying that he loved her. And there were more messages from a man in Italy who said that he didn't love his wife anymore and that he wanted to marry Bee. Bee laughed and said that the potion had never failed her. When I heard that I was sure that she wasn't from Thailand. Magic like that doesn't happen in Thailand but I have heard of it happening in Laos and Cambodia.

On our way home, Sandra said that she thought Bee was stupid and that there would be big problems if she worked on her own. There were robbers who robbed working girls who worked alone and sometimes the immigration people would go to check their visas. It was safer being with an agency, she said. I could see that she was worried but I didn't know what to say to make her feel better. She said she would tell Oliver that Bee was planning to work on her own. I didn't think that was fair but I didn't say anything. Actually, I would be happy if Bee left the agency because then the only girl who will be earning more than me will be Alice.

Something very funny happened when I got back to my flat. Oliver rang me to say that a customer wanted to book me for two hours and that he wanted me to wear my rubber dress. The red one that shows my breasts. I said okay, even though I didn't like wearing it. It's really hard to get on and it feels so uncomfortable. I have to use lots of talcum powder to get it on and it sticks to my skin. Ten minutes later Oliver phoned again to say that the customer also wanted me to wear the thigh-length boots I have. I'm wearing them in some of the photographs on the agency's website. They're made of shiny plastic and they have very high heels. I said okay. Then ten minutes later Oliver phoned again asking if I still have the dog collar. In one of the photographs I'm wearing a dog collar with spikes on it. It was Cat's idea. She said it was sexy. I told Oliver that I didn't have the dog collar, it belonged to the photographer, and Oliver said okay. Then five minutes later he phoned me back. The customer had cancelled. I didn't understand it. I had the dress, I had the boots, but because I didn't have the dog collar he cancelled? Oliver said it was because the customer wanted me to crawl around in the boots and the dress and bark like a dog. I laughed so much. I mean, how crazy can some men be?

I didn't worry too much because I had three customers one after the other, one at two o'clock, one at half past three and one at five o'clock. I think I am busy because Nancy and Sandra have their periods again. Then at seven o'clock Oliver rang me to say that Robert had booked me for four hours outcall. Just as I was getting ready to go to Robert's house I got a text from Simon. He said that he'd tried to book me but the agency said I was busy. I sent him a text back saying I was sorry but that I would be available tomorrow and that I missed him. I always say 'available' and I never say 'I am free' because then the customer might get the wrong idea. I am never free. I am a working girl and men have to pay to see me. Then I sent Robert a text message. 'I am coming now, Daddy,' I said. 'I will be a good girl for you.' I wished that I had had some of Bee's magic potion, then I would have Robert as my customer for ever.

Chapter 32

Thursday May 7. Vince came to see me again yesterday. It was so funny. He booked me under the name James like he did last time but I remembered him straight away because of his shaved head and the 'LOVE' and 'HATE' tattoos on his knuckles. He took out his roll of £50 notes and gave me three and then he asked me for a beer. I gave him a can of Carlsberg and we sat on the sofa. I was dressed in stockings and suspenders that I had bought from Anne Summers. He kept frowning and looking around the apartment and eventually he asked me if he'd been there before. I laughed and said yes, he'd come to see me but that he'd been really drunk. He laughed. He had a nice laugh. He looked a bit scary but actually he was a nice man. He was a good kisser, too. We kissed on the sofa for about ten minutes and then we went into the bedroom. I was very surprised at the way he made love. He was very soft and gentle and kept kissing my neck and whispering sweet words.

Afterwards we lay in bed talking. He was quite funny. He sells drugs. He used to sell just cannabis but he said the price had fallen a lot so it was harder to make a good profit so now he sells cocaine and heroin too. He said that if any of my customers wanted drugs I could phone him and he would deliver. He said he was like Domino's pizza and that if he didn't deliver within thirty minutes it was free. I didn't understand and he said that he was joking. Domino's is a pizza company in London and if they take more than thirty minutes then they give you the pizza free. Vince doesn't give his drugs for free, though. That was a joke.

He said Covid had been really good for him. People had to stay in and that meant they were bored and bored people use a lot of drugs. They would call them and he would deliver. He had a Deliveroo jacket and a Deliveroo sign on his bike and no one suspects that he is delivering drugs. And he said the police don't care because all they care about is people not obeying the Covid rules. If they think that a hairdresser is open they will send a dozen policemen to close it down. But they do nothing about Vince delivering drugs.

Some of my customers do ask if I have drugs but I always say no. It's usually Americans who ask me and they want cocaine. Vince said he would sell to me at a good price and then I could charge the Americans what I wanted because they wouldn't know how much drugs cost in London. He gave me his business card. It said PIZZAMAN and had a mobile phone number. Vince said he was the Pizzaman.

I actually liked Vince. He was so different from the way he looked. I suppose it is like people say, you cannot judge a book by its cover. We talked about that expression last time I was at school. It means things aren't always the way they appear. It's like when I used to walk into a hotel. I would be dressed well and carry an expensive handbag and so everyone assumess that I am a rich tourist. I think a lot of people would look at Vince and think that he was a dangerous thug but in fact he is really nice and quite gentle.

I told Vince that we were alike in that we both sold people what they wanted but that really we were breaking the law when we did it. He laughed and said that there was a big difference because actually prostitution wasn't illegal. I said he was wrong because if it was legal then more people would be doing it. Vince said that in fact being a prostitute isn't against the law in England. It's okay for a man to pay for sex with a girl, there is nothing illegal about that. What is illegal is if a girl goes around offering sex for money. That is illegal which is why the police don't want prostitutes walking on the streets. One girl working on her own was okay, but Vince said that if there was more than one girl working in the same flat then it was called a brothel and that was against the law. I said that was why Oliver said that we all had to have our own apartments.

Vince asked me some questions about Oliver but I said I'd better not talk about him and Vince said that he understood. He said that sometimes the police did arrest the people who ran the agencies because they were pimps. I said that Oliver wasn't a pimp, he just found customers for us. Vince thought that was funny. He said a pimp was someone who controlled prostitutes and that included the people who ran escort agencies. So the police could arrest Oliver if they wanted, but not me. But Vince said the police didn't bother prosecuting escort agencies because they were happy that the girls weren't walking the streets. Vince seems to know a lot about working girls. He seems to know a lot about everything. It was funny because when I was talking to him I didn't feel like I was talking to a customer. He was more like a friend. And he made me laugh. He asked me if I wanted some cocaine and I said no. I have never taken drugs, ever. Some of my friends in Udon Thani took ecstasy and some smoked Ya Bar, but I have never taken drugs and I don't think I ever will. In Thailand they kill people for selling drugs.

Chapter 33

Saturday May 9. Simon came to see me in the evening. He had booked me for three hours this time, and he brought sushi with him. We ate the sushi and watched a horror movie on Netflix. Because Simon had booked me for three hours we had time to make love which was okay, but Simon is so small that I always worry about the condom slipping off. I don't take the pill and I am really scared about getting pregnant. Afterwards he asked me if I would be his girlfriend. He isn't the first customer to ask that. I always say the same thing. I am not doing this job because I want a boyfriend, I am doing this job because I want to make money. A lot of money. Simon said that he wanted to marry me and take care of me. He said he didn't like me doing this job and that he wanted me to only make love to him. He wanted me to be his wife and to have children with him, which is sweet, but I don't want a husband or a boyfriend or another child. I want money. I told Simon that I can earn more than £3,000 a week at the agency so if someone wanted to really take care of me they would have to pay me £150,000 a year. He thought I was joking but I wasn't. If he was serious about wanting to take care of me and could pay me £150,000 then maybe I might stop work. But I don't think he can afford that.

He wanted to book me for another hour but Oliver had already told me that I had a customer for eleven o'clock so he had to go. Simon seemed sad when he left, but that's not my fault. It's not as if he met me in a pub or in a shop, he met me because he saw me on the agency's website and booked me so he can't complain that I am working as an escort.

The customer who came at eleven was an Arab, I think, but he was very white so I didn't mind. He was actually quite nice and polite and he showered for a very long time. He didn't want a bath with me, he just wanted a massage and oral sex. I think he was married. A lot of married men don't want full sex with a working girl because I think they are scared that they might get sick. Actually we are very careful. I never have sex without a condom. He said he worked in London and that he would come to see me again so I gave him my phone number. He wanted to know if he could call me if he wanted to see me but I told him that he would have to book me through the agency.

Oliver phoned me again at two o'clock in the morning and asked me if I would work with Nancy. A customer had booked two girls for two-thirty and he had wanted Nancy and Wanda but Wanda's period had come so she couldn't work. At first I said I didn't want to do it but Oliver said that I would be doing him a big favour and he didn't want to upset a good customer. He saw girls from the agency every week and was a good tipper. I wasn't sure if I could do it, but Nancy is my friend so I thought that perhaps it wouldn't be too bad. I put on my stockings and suspenders and high heels and put my Kenzo coat on top and went to Nancy's apartment. She was wearing a dress made out of mesh which showed off all her body and high heels. She had lots of lipstick and mascara on and looked very sexy. I told her how shy I was about being with her and a customer and she said not to worry, it was like being a movie star. You just had to pretend.

Chapter 34

Tuesday May 12. I lost so much money at the Sloane Square flat on Sunday night. Well actually it was Sunday night and most of Monday. We just kept playing and playing. We didn't stop playing until after mid-day on Monday which means that we played cards for more than twelve hours. At one point I was up £600 and then I was losing and then I was winning £400 but when we finally finished playing I had lost £1,300. Most of the girls lost money but no one lost as much as me. I don't know why I'm not lucky any more. Oliver won a lot. He's always lucky.

A new girl has started working for the agency. Her name is Rachel. At least that is her working name. She is from Surin. She is very pretty with very dark skin and high cheekbones like a lot of girls from Surin. She has a really good body and I think she is the type of girl that farangs like. In Thailand, men prefer girls with white skin and round faces, but farangs seem to like darker skin and long faces. She has a tattoo of a scorpion which is a bit scary. I don't like tattoos and I would never have one. I think they are ugly. It looks good on Rachel, though. It makes her look exotic. She has only just arrived in London and she paid for her own contract. That means she paid £6,000 in Thailand to get a visa and a ticket and I think it was her agent who fixed up the job with Oliver.

She is good fun. She is what we Thai people call San-nuk. San-nuk means fun. She likes to drink and dance and before we played cards she danced sexily while we sang karaoke. She is a very sexy dancer. She told us that she used to dance in a go-go bar called Angle Witch in Nana Plaza. Nana Plaza is a bar area in Bangkok where a lot of prostitutes work. I have never been there but I have heard about it. Rachel said there were more than thirty bars in Nana Plaza and more than five thousand girls working there. Can you believe that? Five thousand girls! They aren't all go-go dancers like she was but she said that almost all of the girls in Nana Plaza will go with customers. She said Angel Witch was one of the busiest bars in Nana Plaza and that the prettiest girls worked there. She said they all dressed in black and they did sexy shows that got the customers really horny. Rachel said that if a customer wanted to take her out of the bar he would pay about £10 and then he would pay the girl about another £30. That means a customer pays just £40 for sex. I am glad I am not a working girl in Thailand, that's for sure.

Rachel said she earned lots of money at the bar which is why she was able to save enough money to buy her own contract. She had tried to get a student visa on her own but the embassy had turned her down because she had no one to sponsor her. She said her plan was to work really hard for one year in London to make enough money to build a house in Surin and then she would go back and work at Angel Witch.

Cat cooked Pad Thai for us and Wanda had brought tubs of Häagen Dazs ice cream and Candy had brought strawberries so we had lots to eat. Oliver asked me if I'd enjoyed working with Nancy and Nancy said that it had been fun. Oliver said we should get some pictures of me and Nancy for the website because some customers really liked to see two girls together. I said okay, because two girls with one man is half the work, really, and so it's easy money.

Bee didn't come to the flat. I suppose because she hadn't been working she didn't have any more for Oliver so she didn't want to come. I don't think it was because she was scared of Alice. I don't think Bee is scared of anybody. Nancy said that Bee's picture is still on the website so that when people phone up for her Oliver tries to get the customer to take another girl.

I went home in an Uber taxi with Nancy and Sandra. Sandra said she was a bit worried about Bee and wanted us to go to see her but Nancy and I both said we were too tired. Sandra said we could maybe go around in the week and we said yes. I think she's a bit worried that Bee might disappear because if she disappears then Sandra will lose the money she paid to bring Bee to London.

When I got home I slept almost the whole day but then Oliver phoned just after six o'clock in the evening to tell me that Robert had booked me for four hours. I was so happy.

Chapter 35

Wednesday May 13. Cat took me and Nancy to get new photographs taken yesterday. I went to see Nancy first. Chris was there and he asked if he could come with us but Nancy said no, she didn't want Cat to know that she had a ik. When Cat phoned to say that she was outside in the taxi, Chris asked Nancy if she would give him some money and she gave him £100. I don't understand why she gives him money. He's supposed to be her boyfriend. I think she is crazy to have FFF with him but she is even crazier to give him money. Nancy told me not to tell Cat about Chris but I knew that already. I don't think Cat or Oliver would be happy to know that she had a boyfriend and that he was the reason she wasn't working very hard.

The shop still had the CLOSED sign on the door but Cat rang the bell and the photographer opened it. It was Thomas the gay guy who took our photographs the last time we were there. I think he takes all the pictures for the agency. Cat said we had to pay £200 each for the new photographs. Nancy said she didn't have any money so she asked me if I would lend it to her and I said okay. While we were changing, I heard Thomas talking to Cat about Bee. Thomas said that Bee had phoned him asking if he would let her have copies of the photographs he had taken of her. She wanted them on a disc but she didn't say why she wanted them. Thomas wanted to know if it was okay to give her the pictures but Cat said that it wasn't okay because the pictures belonged to the agency. Actually that isn't fair because the girls have to pay for their own photographs so really they belong to us. But I think Cat knows that Bee wants the photographs because she wants her own website. I think Bee can't take new photographs now because her eye looks so bad. I could see that Cat was a bit angry and she told Thomas he must never give the photographs to Bee and if she wanted him to take new photographs then he had to say no. I think Thomas will do what Cat says because she gives him a lot of business.

Thomas took a lot of photographs of me and Nancy together. Some of the pictures were very sexy, with me and Nancy kissing and touching each other. In one of them I am on my hands and knees wearing the spiky dog collar and she is holding my lead like I am her dog. Sometimes it felt funny and we giggled a lot until Thomas scolded us and said that we had to be professional. Some of the things he made us do seemed silly at the time but when we saw the photographs we realised what he had meant. Nancy and me did look very sexy together, like we really enjoyed being with each other.

Afterwards Cat said she was going to see Oliver so Nancy and I went back home in an Uber taxi together. In the taxi Nancy asked me if I would lend her some money. I asked her why and she said that she was just short of money this week because she had paid her rent and her council tax. I asked her how much she wanted and she said £2,000. That seemed like a lot of money but she isn't earning a lot now that she is with Chris so much, and she loses a lot at cards. So I gave her another £2,000 which means that she owes me £2,200. I think it is crazy that a working girl can sleep with men for £150 an hour but then she has to borrow money, but I didn't say anything. I just hope that she remembers to pay me back.

Chapter 36

Thursday May 14. I don't understand why men think they can have a working girl as a girlfriend. They look at a website and choose a girl because they want to have sex with her, right? So they must understand that the girl is selling sex for money and that that's their job. So why then do they think that the girl would want to be their girlfriend? If I was looking for a boyfriend or a husband, I wouldn't be working as an escort. I work as an escort because I want to make a lot of money quickly.

When I worked as a waitress in a Thai restaurant, lots of guys wanted to be my boyfriend. I could always tell the ones that wanted to ask me out. Usually the first time they would come in a group, but they would smile a lot and maybe ask my name. Then they would come in again, probably with someone else, and this time they would give me a business card and tell me that they wanted me to call them. I never did, not even if the guy was good looking. Then they would start coming in on their own and eat alone, trying to talk to me whenever I went by their table. Then finally maybe they would ask me out for a meal or to go to see a movie, but I always said no. I had to work six nights a week and I never finished before one o'clock in the morning. Then during the day I was at school. I didn't have time for a boyfriend. Once I said no to a guy, he would stop coming in. The manager of the restaurant noticed that a lot of customers were coming in to the restaurant because I was there and he said that I should flirt with them, but even if I did they always stopped coming in once I turned them down.

I understood why guys would ask me out when I was a waitress, but I didn't understand why they thought I would want to go for a meal as a date, because I worked in a restaurant! But I don't understand why my customers now think that I would want to go out with them. Simon keeps sending me messages asking me if I want to go and see a movie with him and I just ignore him. The first time he asked I said that he'd have to book me through the agency but he said that he wanted to go on a real date. He doesn't seem to get it, booking me through the agency would be a real date. He could book me for three hours outcall and we could go and see a movie and that would be a date. He knows I'm working, so why does he think that I would go out with him for free? I'm not like Nancy. I would never FFF.

A lot of customers ask me out now. Probably four or five a week. It's usually guys who have been to see me three or four times. Sometimes they ask me out straight away, the first time they see me. They have sex with me and then they ask mc if I want to go and scc a movie some time. How stupid is that? But most of the ones who ask me out wait until the third or fourth time. Usually they bring me a present, some flowers or chocolates or perfume. Then they sweet talk me, then they ask me out. I always say that I'd love to go out with them but that the agency won't let me and then they always say that the agency needn't know. Do they think I'm stupid? Sometimes after I've turned them down I never see them again. But others, like Simon, keep on asking. They don't give up. In a way it's good because they're regular customers but it can get a bit boring when they keep asking and asking and asking.

Even if I was looking for a boyfriend or a husband, why would a customer think that I would want him? Why would I want a boyfriend who visits prostitutes? If he met me through the agency then he's probably been to see lots of agency girls. I don't want a man who visits prostitutes. And if let a customer be my boyfriend, how could I ever trust him? I'd know that if he ever got bored with me he'd start looking at the agency websites again. No, I would never want a customer as a boyfriend. And I don't understand why a customer would want an agency girl as his wife. Surely every time he looked at her he'd think about all the men she'd slept with. Do you know, if a girl works for an agency for one year she has probably had sex with more than five hundred men? Why would a man want a wife who has had sex with five hundred men? That's just crazy. No, I will wait until I have finished doing this job before I look for a husband. And I will never, ever, ever, ever, tell him that I worked as an escort girl. That will be a secret for ever.

Chapter 37

Saturday May 16. The new pictures of me and Nancy went up on the website on Wednesday night and yesterday we had two customers who wanted to see us together. The first was a man called Elliot who wanted an hour's incall so I went around to Nancy's apartment because hers is a bit bigger than mine. This time she had on a sexy black plastic dress with holes cut out for her breasts and I was wearing red stockings and suspenders that I had bought from Anne Summers. Chris was in the apartment and he said that we both looked really sexy. Actually I didn't like him looking at me. I know that sounds a bit silly because customers see me naked all the time but he isn't a customer, he's Nancy's kik, and I don't think that he should be looking at me. Nancy didn't mind, though, so I didn't say anything, but I put a towel around me and told Nancy that I was a bit cold.

The downstairs bell rang at just before two o'clock and we looked at the customer on the CCTV and then Chris left. Before he went he asked Nancy for some money and she gave him £50. I really don't understand Nancy. Not only does she FFF but she gives him money, too.

Elliot was about forty years old and quite thin with blond hair that I think was dyed. He smelt of cigarettes and I think he had been drinking whisky. We sat on the sofa and both kissed him. Nancy has a big shower so we both went into the shower with him. We both made sure that he was really clean and then Nancy knelt down and gave him oral sex while I kissed him on the mouth. He tasted quite bad, really, because of the cigarettes. Nancy was really clever. She got him really hard and then she looked up at him and said that she wanted him to come in her mouth. We dried Elliott and took him into the bedroom. We gave him a massage but he couldn't get hard again. That was why Nancy was so clever. A lot of men when they get a bit old can only come one time, unless they cheat and take Viagra of course! So when he came in her mouth in the shower, that was all he could do. We just gave him a massage in the bedroom and then he went. He didn't tip us, but that was okay. He had paid us £300 and he hadn't even had sex with either of us. I wish we had more customers like that. I don't mind having sex with customers and sometimes it can be fun, but when you are busy it can hurt a bit if you do it too much.

After Elliott had gone Chris came back. He started kissing Nancy and said that he wanted to go into the bedroom with her. Nancy laughed and said that he was always horny but she went with him anyway. I went home and showered and watched a Netflix movie.

Oliver phoned me to say that I had a customer at four o'clock, incall for an hour and a half. His name was Tom and he was quite good-looking, about thirty years old, I think. He said that he had been to Thailand many times. He said he had been to Pattaya most but that he really liked Phuket, where the beaches are good. Phuket is too expensive for most Thai people, it is mainly farangs who go there. Tom said that he wanted a Thai girlfriend but that all Thai girls cared about was money. That didn't seem fair to me. Not all Thai girls care about money. We are like girls everywhere, we want a man to love us and take care of us, a man who can make us happy and feel safe. Then he said that all Thai girls lie and that's not true at all. I think maybe Tom just talks to bargirls and of course they will lie because they want his money. Thai people have a saying – Farang Ru Mak Mai Dee. It means that the farang who knows too much isn't a good thing. Tom thinks he knows too much about Thai people but really he doesn't. I didn't like it when he said bad things about Thai people. I kept smiling at him and being cute with him but really I hated him. He asked me if I would give him my phone number but I told him that my agency wouldn't let me do that. He had sex with me twice and I pretended to come both times but really I didn't like being with him at all.

Chapter 38

Sunday May 17. Today I went to Sandra's flat to eat some Tom Yum Pla that she had cooked. It's spicy fish soup just like the soup that my mother used to cook. There was another Thai girl there. Her name was Dao and she was quite young, just twenty-two years old, small and pretty with very long hair. Dao is a student like me but she also worked as a waitress at one of the restaurants that Sandra used to eat in. They only do takeaway now so they don't need waitresses. She was only paid in cash so they just sacked her when Covid started and she gets no money from the Government.

Sandra was very clever. She kept saying how expensive London was and how the people who worked in restaurants earned very little money. Dao said that it was hard work and that she never had enough money even before Covid. The owner of the restaurant where she worked kept all the tips for herself so Dao only had her wages and she was only paid £8 an hour. Sandra laughed and said she earned £100 an hour. Dao wanted to know how Sandra earned £100 an hour and Sandra explained about the agency. It was funny because I realised it was what she'd told me, the time she and her boyfriend had come to see me at my restaurant in Camden. She said that it was easy work, that you spent time with wealthy farangs and were nice to them, that you got to live in a nice apartment and go to nice hotels and wear nice clothes. Dao had some questions, but I could tell that she was interested. Then she asked me if I did the same job, and I said that I did. She asked me what it was like, sleeping with farangs, and I said that actually it was sometimes good fun.

Dao said she wanted to try. I asked her if she was sure she could do it and she said that actually she had done things for money when she was a student in Sara Buri. She said there was a road in Sara Buri where students waited for men. Men would drive up and the girls would get in the car and they would drive somewhere quiet and the girl would give the man oral sex for 500 baht or maybe 1,000 baht.

Sometimes the girls would have sex with the man but Dao said she never did, she just did oral. She said she was sixteen when she did it the first time because she wanted a new mobile phone and her father wouldn't give her enough money. She said a lot of her friends were doing it, too. Sandra said she could come with us to the Sloane Square flat on Sunday to meet Oliver and Cat and they could talk to her about working for the agency.

Then we got an Uber taxi back to Bayswater. Dao had to go and see a friend but Sandra came back to my apartment with me. She said she was sure that Dao would do really well as an escort girl and she was short of money now that her restaurant had closed because of Covid. She went into my bedroom and saw that I had done what she suggested and hung a mirror at the end of the bed. It was a good idea because it made customers horny to see themselves making love to me and when they are horny they come quicker. Sandra said she had put a television and a DVD player in her bedroom as well so that she could play sexy movies because that made customers horny, too.

Sandra said that she was really angry at Bee. Bee had either turned off her mobile phone or she had thrown away the SIM card. And she hadn't paid Sandra any money for two weeks. Sandra asked me if I would go with her to talk to Bee and I said that maybe I would next week. Actually I do not want to get involved. If Sandra has a problem with Bee then that is her problem. I do not want to get into a fight with Bee. In fact I do not want to get into a fight with anyone. I just want to earn money. I understand that Sandra is worried that Bee might not pay her back, but that's not my problem.

Then I was really surprised because Sandra asked me if I would lend her some money. Sandra earns a lot of money and has a lot of regular customers. She is never the top earning girl at the agency, but she is never the worst either. And she has been working for a long time so she should have saved a lot of money by now. Sandra said she needed £3,000 and could I help her. I asked her if she had a problem and she said that it wasn't really her who needed the money, it was her boyfriend. She has been helping him pay for his Porsche and he didn't have any money this month. I couldn't believe it. She was helping him pay for his car? What sort of boyfriend is that? Sandra always said how rich her boyfriend was and how well-dressed he was and how much he spent on presents for her, but now I think that maybe it's her money that's paying for it all. I think she is crazy but she is my friend so I said I would help her so I got £3,000 for her. Actually I have a lot of money in my apartment. More than £15,000. I send a lot back to Kung and some I post to my mum in Udon Thani but the rest I keep in my room. I don't have a bank account in London and I'm not sure how to open one. I am worried that they might ask questions about where I am getting my money from.

Anyway, I keep my money in envelopes under the carpet behind the sofa. I don't think anyone will ever find it there. I put one thousand pounds in each envelope and I lay them flat under the carpet. I think it's a safe hiding place. I gave three envelopes to Sandra and she said she would pay me back in a week or two. I hope she doesn't forget.

Chapter 39

Monday May 18. Sandra and I took Dao to meet Oliver on Sunday evening. Alice was the best earning girl last week so she was very happy. Dao stared at all the money we gave to Oliver like it was a dream. She said she had never seen so much money at one time. She kept asking questions about what it was like to be a working girl, and Cat said they could go and take photographs on Wednesday if she wanted. Dao said she would but she wanted to know if they could hide her face. Oliver said no because customers thought that if a girl hid her face it was because she was ugly. He said Dao didn't have to worry because no one in Thailand ever saw the websites. Cat said Dao should have a working name so we all talked about it and decided on Laura. Cat said she would lend Dao some money for clothes and for a new apartment, same as she did when I started work. I hope that Dao realises that once she has the apartment and the clothes she has no choice, she will have to do this job so that she can pay back Cat and Oliver. In a way it is a trap. But I think she really wants to do the job. I know she really wants the money.

Chapter 40

Tuesday May 19. Yesterday a policeman came to talk to me. He was actually quite nice but when he first said who he was I was crying and begging him not to take me to jail. Looking back it was quite funny but at the time I was really upset. He had booked me for one hour's incall at two o'clock and Oliver said his name was Neil. He was about ten minutes late. He was about thirty, tall with very dark brown hair and blue eyes and he was wearing a suit and carrying a briefcase. He looked like a businessman. I was wearing my white vinyl nurse's outfit and white high heels and I looked really cute. I kissed him on the cheek and asked him if he wanted a drink and he said he'd have an orange juice. He sat down on the sofa and when I took him his drink he opened a wallet and showed me his ID card and said that he was a police officer. I was so shocked I dropped the orange juice and it went all over the floor. Some of it splashed on his trousers. That's when I started crying. I begged him not to put me in jail or to send me back to Thailand. Tears were running down my face and I was shaking.

He said that it was okay, he wasn't there to arrest me. He told me to sit down and then he got a cloth from the kitchen and cleaned up the orange juice. He said that he worked for the Metropolitan Police's Human Trafficking Command who are the police who look after working girls in London. He asked me if I was being forced to work. I told him it was my choice, I wanted to work so that I could help my family. He asked me if anyone had brought me to London and I said no, I had come on my own, but I didn't tell him about Kung. I started crying again and he said I wasn't in trouble, he was there because he wanted to help me and the other girls at the agency. He took out some photographs to show me. He said that a man had been robbing working girls, beating them up and stealing their money. One of the girls was still in hospital, he said.

Some of the photographs were from CCTV cameras but they weren't very clear, just a man in a padded jacket with a baseball cap so you couldn't see his face. One of the photographs was a computer picture of what the man looked like. He was black with very short hair and a flat nose. I hadn't seen him before. The policeman gave me a folder containing copies of the photographs and he gave me some business cards with his telephone number on and asked me if I'd show the rest of the girls at the agency the pictures and if anyone recognised the man to give him a call.

I was so relieved that I wanted to kiss him. I started crying again, but this time because I was so happy that he wasn't going to put me in prison. I asked him why he hadn't spoken to Oliver and he said that usually the people who ran the agencies didn't want to talk to the police. They were scared that the police wanted to put them out of business. I asked him if it was true that the bosses of the agency could be sent to prison and he said yes because they were living off the earnings of prostitutes. But he said that usually the police didn't bother about the bosses of the agencies unless they were using illegal immigrants or they were abusing the girls. I said that actually Oliver was a nice man.

Neil said that I should always check on the CCTV camera that I could see a customer's face. The building kept tapes of the CCTV pictures so if someone was going to steal he wouldn't risk showing his face. I said that I always did that.

Neil seemed like a nice man. I asked him if it was true that working girls in their own flats weren't breaking the law and he said that it was. Providing the neighbours didn't complain he said the police didn't bother about girls in flats. If there was more than one girl and a maid then the police might say that it was a brothel, but even then they wouldn't do anything unless somebody complained. He said that might change because of Covid. People weren't supposed to visit the flats of people they didn't know, but again the police would only investigate if someone complained.

Sometimes the police helped immigration if they wanted to round up illegal immigrants. I said that all the girls at our agency had visas, but that was a lie because several of the girls including Alice and Nancy have overstayed. Then Neil said he was going to go. I asked him if he was going to pay me and he said he wasn't, which I didn't think was fair because I would have to pay Oliver his commission which was £50. But I didn't say anything, I just smiled and said goodbye.

After he had gone I phoned Sandra and told her what had happened. She said it wouldn't be a good idea to tell Oliver because he wouldn't be happy that I had been talking to a policeman. She said it would be better if we showed the pictures to the girls. I think she might be right. I asked her if she could pay me back some of the money she owed me and she said she hadn't been very busy on Monday but maybe she could pay me back something by the end of the week. She said she was short of money because Bee hadn't paid her back but I think it's because she is giving all her money to her boyfriend.

Chapter 41

Thursday May 21. Yesterday I went with Dao to get her website photographs taken. Dao and I got an Uber taxi to the photographers and Cat was already waiting. Cat had some very sexy outfits for Dao and she got her to try them on. There was a schoolgirl's uniform with a tartan skirt and a tight white shirt, a nurse's outfit like the one I have, white bra and suspenders that looked really good, a black bra and suspenders set like I have, a red dress that showed off her breasts, and a body suit made of fishnet material that showed off all her body. It was funny because I thought Dao would be shy but she wasn't at all and she walked around like a model and made us all laugh. She has a very good body. She is quite short, about five feet two, I think, and has a very small waist so that her breasts look quite big.

Cat said Dao should buy all the clothes because they looked so sexy, and that Dao could owe her the £450 they cost and another £200 for the photographs. That is £650 that Dao owes Cat already. That means she will have to have sex seven times to pay back the money. And Cat said she was going to show her an apartment near Marble Arch that cost £1,800 a month. Cat said she would pay for the deposit and the first month's rent. Dao didn't seem worried at all. Actually I think she will be very good at this job.

Something very strange happened while Thomas was taking the photographs. Cat was helping him get Dao to look sexy, and while they were busy Cat's mobile phone rang. Well, it didn't ring because it was set to silent but it flashed and the name of the caller came up. It was Kung. Now Kung is a common name in Thailand. It can be a name for a girl or for a boy. Actually it is not a real name, it is a nickname. It means Prawn. It could have been anyone called Kung phoning Cat, but I got a very strange feeling, like when you know that something bad is going to happen. When the phone stopped flashing I checked the number and do you know what? It was my boyfriend. It was my Kung calling Cat. How could he know about Cat? He doesn't know what job I am doing, he doesn't know that I work for Cat's agency. Why would he call Cat? And why wouldn't he tell me that he knows Cat? I was very worried. A bit scared, actually.

Then Cat came over and I tried to smile because I didn't want her to know how worried I was. Cat said she had an idea. She said that I should let Thomas take some photographs of me and Dao together. She said we were both sexy girls and that we would get more business if we worked together. Dao said she was happy so I said okay, but it meant that I had to pay another £200 for the photographs. I found it difficult to look sexy in the pictures because I was so worried about the phone call and Thomas kept scolding me.

After Thomas had taken the pictures, Cat took Dao to see the apartment in Marble Arch and I went home in a taxi. I was busy all day which was good because it stopped me thinking about the phone call. Kung called me five times and I ignored him but he called again and I answered. He was asking for more money and I said I would send him some by Western Union but I didn't tell him that I knew he had phoned Cat. Something is wrong but I do not know what it is.

I had four incall customers between two o'clock and eight o'clock, two for one hour and two for ninety minutes, then Oliver phoned to say that Robert wanted me for four hours. I was so happy that I was going to see Robert because he is kind and gentle and I don't have to have sex with him. It was a good day. I earned £1,440 and I get to keep £960 plus I got some tips. I didn't get home until three o'clock in the morning and I was so tired but I couldn't sleep. I was thinking too much.

Chapter 42

Friday May 22. Dao phoned me this morning. She was really excited. She said her apartment was really nice and she wanted me to see it. It wasn't far from my flat so I walked there. It is a nice flat. It is bigger than mine and has an extra bedroom though it is quite small. But it means that she doesn't have to sleep in the bed where she works, which is a good thing, I think. I don't like sleeping in my bed and most nights I sleep on the sofa in the living room. My bed is where I work, it's not where I sleep. Dao said she was really excited about working. Her pictures weren't on the website yet but Oliver had said that he would send her customers anyway. Bee's pictures are still on the website and so are other girls who left a long time ago. She had made her bedroom look really nice and she had a Buddha figure on top of her wardrobe with some flowers and candles and there was a poster of a Thai temple on the back of her door.

She had boxes of condoms ready and KY jelly and there was lots of shampoo and soap in the bathroom. She said Cat had been shopping with her and told her what to buy. She had taken a mirror from the living room and put it against the wall at the end of the bed and I knew that had been Sandra's idea.

She asked me what it was like, the first time that I had been with a customer. I said that I had cried, but that really it hadn't been that bad. Most customers were nice and if a customer wasn't nice you just had to think about something else. If I'm with a customer and I don't like him then I just think about shopping.

Chapter 43

Saturday May 23. I can't believe what happened yesterday. I had someone very famous as my customer. Very famous! If I say who it was, everyone would know. He is a famous actor from America, very handsome and very cute! He had booked me and Nancy together for two hours incall at Nancy's apartment and he had used the name David, but that wasn't his real name. Chris was at Nancy's apartment again and he kept looking at me in the way I don't like. I don't know why Nancy lets him stay there all the time. Actually I do, she does not like being on her own. I am the same, but I do not have a kik to keep me company. Anyway, Nancy gave Chris £50 and he went to the pub while we waited for David. When he rang the bell we looked through the CCTV camera and he was wearing sunglasses and a baseball cap but when we opened the front door we knew who he was right away.

He was laughing because he knew that we had recognised him. He said he was in London to talk about his new movie with a producer here. And what was really funny was that I had been watching one of his movies on Netflix on Thursday. I had been watching him on the screen and now he was in Nancy's apartment and we were going to make love to him. It was crazy. There are lots of girls who would give anything to be in bed with this man and he was paying us to have sex with him. Nancy was really excited and started kissing him right away. I asked him what he wanted to drink and he said anything would be okay. Nancy had a bottle of champagne in the fridge so I opened it and she had chocolates and strawberries in the fridge so I put them on the table for him.

Nancy sat down with him on the sofa and undid his trousers and gave him oral sex and I took off my bra so that he could kiss my breasts. I couldn't believe what was happening. He is so famous, and he has a wife and his wife is a famous actress too. His wife is very beautiful and I don't know why he would want to be with two working girls when he has such a beautiful wife. He started kissing me and he was a really good kisser. Nancy took off his trousers and then she went crazy. She told me in Thai that she was going to make love to him without a condom and that maybe she would get pregnant with his baby and then she would be rich. I told her that she was crazy but she took off her panties and started rubbing herself against him and making him really horny. I could see that he really wanted to make love to Nancy and for a moment I thought he was going to make love to her with no condom but then he pushed her off, laughing. He said he had to shower. I gave him a towel and he asked us if we had any cocaine. I said no but I could get some for £400. He asked me if it was okay to pay in dollars and I said sure and he gave me $800. He went into the shower with Nancy and I phoned Vince. Vince said he wasn't far away and that he'd come around to the flat with the cocaine.

I went into the bathroom and got into the shower. Nancy was soaping him and kissing him and I helped. We both gave him oral in the shower and then Nancy started rubbing herself against him. She turned around and bent down and I could see that she was trying to get him to make love to her but he pushed her away and said that he had to wear a condom.

We both used towels to dry him and then we took him to the bedroom. Nancy gave him oral again while I kissed him. Then the bell rang. It was Vince. I put on a robe and opened the door and gave him £300 and he gave me the cocaine. He winked at me and said I looked sexy and that maybe he would come and see me later if he wasn't too busy.

When I went back to the bedroom, Nancy was doing 69 with the customer but they stopped and the customer took some cocaine and gave some to Nancy. He asked if I wanted some but I said no, then Nancy said that I didn't sniff cocaine but I would lick it off her pussy. He said he wanted to see that. I was a bit angry at Nancy but I did it because I had already done it before. This time Nancy put a lot on her pussy and she held my head tightly while I licked her and then while I was doing it, he made love to me, doggy-style. It actually felt quite good and I think this time the cocaine did affect me a bit.

Nancy pushed me away and said that she wanted to make love to him so I took off the condom. Nancy got a new condom and she told me to kiss him so that he couldn't see what she was doing. I told her not to be stupid but she said that he wouldn't know. I thought she was crazy but I kissed him and stroked his chest. Nancy opened the condom and pretended to put it on him, but then she pushed him inside her and started to make love to him. Nancy was moaning and telling him to come and I could tell from the way that he was kissing me that he was really horny and then he came. Nancy pretended to come, too. At least I think she was pretending. Then she got off him. She still had the condom in her hand and she pretended that she had taken it off him but I know that actually he had come inside her. She went to the bathroom and I lay next to him and stroked him.

He said he liked Asian girls but that he could never see Asian girls when he was in America because photographers followed him wherever he went. He said his wife would kill him if ever she found out what he did, and I think he is right. I do not understand why men with beautiful wives want to sleep with working girls.

Nancy came out of the bathroom. She told me that she could feel his sperm inside her and that she was sure she would have a beautiful baby. I told her that she was crazy, even if she got pregnant how would she ever get to talk to him again and she said it wouldn't be a problem, she would get a lawyer in America.

We gave him a massage and then he asked us if we would do a lesbian show for him and we did. We drank more champagne and Nancy asked him if he would send us signed photographs and he said that he would, but I am not sure if he really will.

When he went Nancy and I were laughing and jumping up and down. It was like a dream. I said that we mustn't tell anybody and she said she was going to tell Chris and I said no, no one must know. It wouldn't be fair if anyone knew. We had to be professional. I won't even tell Vince, even though I would love to see his face if I told him who he had sold cocaine to.

Vince didn't come to see me last night, so I suppose he was busy. I did see four customers, though, all of them were incall. None of them were anywhere near as handsome as the famous customer.

Chapter 44

Sunday May 24. Sandra came to my flat to see me yesterday morning, with her boyfriend Andy. She said that Bee had a new website and that she was working on her own and charging £200 an hour as an escort. Actually, that seemed a really good idea. She will be earning twice as much as I earn because she does not have to pay an agency. After I have paid Oliver his commission I get £100 an hour. Bee will get to keep all of her £200. Sandra said that she had been to Bee's flat in South Kensington but she wasn't there. She had moved. And her old phone number wasn't working. She and Andy had spent hours looking at websites on the internet and they had finally found her. Now she had a different name. She was calling herself Tanya. And she had a different phone number.

Sandra said she was really angry at Bee because she still owed her most of the £18,000 for the contract and she had loaned her £3,000 for her flat which meant that she still owed Sandra about £20,000 which is a lot of money. I used my phone to look at Bee's website and actually it was quite good. The pictures were very sexy and the English was really good even though Bee does not speak very good English. I think somebody must have helped her. Sandra asked me if I would go with her to speak to Bee. I didn't want to but I said I would. Actually I am a bit worried that Sandra will not be able to pay me what she owes me if Bee does not pay her first.

Andy used his phone to call the number on the website and she answered. He asked if he could have two hours incall and she said yes, that would be £380 and she gave him her address. It was as easy as that.

Her new flat is in Gloucester Place, which is near Baker Street. We drove there in Andy's Porsche. He drove very fast and kept stamping on the brakes. People in Thailand do not drive very well but I think they drive better than Andy. I was in the back and I was a bit scared. I do not know why men like to drive Porsches. They are quite small, really.

There was no camera outside the building but there was an intercom and Andy pressed it. Then we heard Bee ask who it was and he said 'Dave' which was the name he had used to make the booking. Then the door buzzed open. Sandra asked Andy if he would wait outside because Bee might worry if she saw him and all she wanted to do was to talk to her and Andy said okay.

Bee's flat is on the third floor so we walked upstairs and rang the bell to her flat. When she opened the door her eyes went wide she was so shocked. I think she was going to shut the door but Sandra pushed it open. Bee was wearing a very sexy red vinyl dress and had high heels and she had on a lot of make up which helped to hide the bruises on her face. She didn't ask what had happened to Dave so I think that she knew that Sandra had tricked her.

Her flat was very nice with tall ceilings and an old-fashioned fireplace. She had a really big sofa and a marble coffee table and there were nice pictures on the wall. I think she must be paying a lot of rent.

Sandra kept smiling but I could see she wasn't happy. Bee made us Chinese tea and brought some small cakes from the kitchen. Bee was asking lots of questions about Oliver and the girls, but I could see that she was a bit worried. Then Sandra asked her about the money that Bee owed her and Bee said that right now she didn't have any because she had used £2,000 to pay for the deposit on the flat and she had to pay a farang to design her website and that had cost £1,000 and she had had to use two photographers because the first photographer had done a really bad job. So far she had had only four customers so she didn't have any money to spare.

Sandra said that Bee wasn't being fair because Sandra had paid a lot of money to bring her to London and she had paid for the apartment in South Kensington. Bee said she had wanted to move because she thought Oliver wouldn't be happy if she worked in the same apartment but I don't think that was true. I think she wanted to move because the new flat was much nicer than the old one.

Sandra asked Bee when she would pay her back some of the money she owed her and Bee said maybe next week. Sandra kept smiling but I could see she was not happy. Thai people often smile even when they are hurt or angry. That is why they call Thailand the Land of Smiles. But sometimes Thai people can be dangerous when they smile.

We drank our tea and ate some cakes and then we left. Bee said that she would phone Sandra when she had some money for her. When we were in the car I spoke to Sandra in Thai so that Andy wouldn't understand what we were saying. First I asked her about the money she owed me. She said she couldn't pay me back yet because she didn't have the money from Bee. Then I asked her about the first time she met me, in the restaurant in Camden. I asked her if she had gone there to eat or if she had gone there to see me. She pretended not to understand what I meant. I said I wanted to know if Cat had told her to go to the restaurant, and if Cat had told her that I worked there. I could see from the look on her face that I was right. Cat had sent her. I think she was going to lie to me but before she could speak I said she had to tell me the truth because it wasn't fair to lie to me. Then she said yes, Cat had told her my name and that I worked at the restaurant and that Cat wanted her to tell me about the agency. Sandra said she didn't want me to tell Cat that I knew and I said of course, I just wanted to know the truth. Sandra said that sometimes Cat saw girls who she knew would be good working girls and she asked Sandra to talk to them, the same as we did with Dao. I said everything was okay and that I was happy working for the agency. Happy with the money, anyway.

When I got back to my flat I had three customers. I can't even remember what they looked like because I was thinking too much about Kung and Cat. Now I think I know everything. Kung wants me to do this job because he wants money from me. He knows Cat because she is from Udon Thani and I think he sent me to London so that I would do this job. I think he told Cat where I worked and Cat sent Sandra to talk to me and to persuade me to work for the agency. It was all a plan. Now I know for sure that Kung does not love me. He sent me to London so that I would work as a prostitute. I don't think he ever really loved me because if he did love me he would not want me to do this job. I hate him now but I am not sure what I should do. We are building the house together in Udon Thani but he did all the paperwork so I do not know if he put it in my name or his. So far the land and the house has cost about three million baht and most of that money has been from me. Now I can not sleep because I am thinking too much. Kung phoned me four times today but I did not answer the phone. I know what he wants. He wants more money.

Chapter 45

Monday May 25. Kung phoned me ten times yesterday but I didn't speak to him, not one time. I am not sure what I should do about him but I know one thing for sure and that is that he does not love me. And I do not want to be his Mia Noi any more. I am not angry with Cat and Oliver because I am happy working as an escort, but I am not happy with Kung because he lied to me.

I had a very good week and when I went to the Sloane Square flat I had £1,900 for Oliver. The big surprise was Dao. It was her first week and she had earned £4,200 and so she had £1,400 for Oliver, the same as Sandra. Cat said that she was a natural and that two customers had already gone back to see her twice. I can see why she does so well because she is always happy and smiling and she seems quite young. I think most customers like young girls. Dao seemed to have changed very quickly. She was laughing and joking and drinking beer and she lost quite a lot of money playing cards. I lost money, too, almost £700, because I couldn't concentrate. Everybody asked me what was wrong but I didn't say. I can't tell anyone about my problem.

Chapter 47

Tuesday May 26. Chris came to see me yesterday. He had booked me through the agency and said that his name was Paul and I didn't see his face on the CCTV and it was too late when I opened the door so I had to let him in. He was laughing and telling me that I looked very surprised which is true, I was. Chris is Nancy's kik and he shouldn't have come to see me. I was wearing my black stocking and suspenders and my Gucci high heels and I had spent ages getting my hair to look nice but when I saw it was Chris I put on my bathrobe. Chris took £150 from his pocket and tried to give it to me but I said that I couldn't do anything with him because he was Nancy's boyfriend. He said that Nancy would never know and that he didn't love her but he really wanted to be with me. What made me really angry was that I was sure that the money he was trying to give me was money that Nancy had given him.

Chris tried to kiss me but I pushed him away. He asked what was wrong because he had money and I told him again, I couldn't do anything because he was Nancy's boyfriend. He got angry then and he grabbed me and pushed me onto the sofa and he tried to have sex with me, but I scratched him and pushed him away. He said I was a hooker so why was I fighting him and I ran to the kitchen and got a knife and said that if he came near me again I'd cut off his dick and throw it out of the window. He called me a lot of names but then he went away. I was so angry that I cried. I can't tell Oliver what happened and I will have to pay him his £50 commission even though I didn't get any money. And I am not sure if I can tell Nancy or not. Maybe she will blame me. Maybe she will think I wanted him to come to see me. Sometimes men can be really unfair. And it wasn't fair to call me a hooker. Just because I am a working girl doesn't mean that I have sex with everybody. And I am sure that I will not have sex with my friend's boyfriend. Never, never, never.

I wish all men could be more like Robert. Robert is always sweet and kind. Not long after Chris left, Oliver phoned me to tell me that Robert had booked me for three hours that evening. Oliver could tell from my voice that I was upset and he asked me if everything was okay and I said I was just a little bit tired.

I had two customers before I went to see Robert. One was a nice young man called John who only wanted oral and who pulled my hair really tightly when he came. He said he worked for the council tax department and if I ever needed help with my tax he would help me and he gave me his phone number. I wondered if he knew Tony, the agency customer with the moustache who worked for the council tax department, but I did not ask him because it would not be professional to talk about another customer. He was wearing a wedding ring so I think he was married. The other customer was older, about sixty, I think, and he couldn't get hard no matter what I did. I gave him a bath and then a massage and then oral but he just would not get hard. I felt a bit sorry for him. His name was Martin and he said his wife had died two years ago and that he had loved her very much. He said that he hadn't been able to have sex since she had died, but that sometimes he just wanted to be close to a woman again. Actually it was a very sad story. I almost made him come but then his hour was up so he had to go because he said he didn't have enough money to stay any longer.

After Martin went I showered and put on my make up and my school uniform because Robert always likes me to wear school uniform when I go to see him. Robert is such a nice man, and always so kind to me. He made me peanut butter sandwiches which now I quite like to eat, and a strawberry milkshake because I like it better than milk on its own. Then he gave me a bath which I also quite like. Usually I give the customer a bath but Robert likes to bathe me and he is very soft and gentle. His bathroom is bigger than my whole apartment and the bath is huge, big enough for three people but he never gets in the bath with me. Then he dried me with a fluffy towel that he said came from Egypt and then he carried me into the bedroom and kissed my feet and licked my toes until he made himself come. I am always so relaxed when I have been with Robert, he actually makes me forget that I am a working girl.

Chapter 46

Thursday May 28. Dao phoned me yesterday afternoon. She was crying because someone had stolen her money and she asked me if I would go around to her flat so I said that I would. It was quiet and I hadn't had any customers though Simon had booked me for three hours starting at 8pm so I knew that I would be watching a movie and eating either Chinese food or a pizza.

Dao was still crying when I got to her flat. The customer who had taken her money was called Ronnie. She said he was quite nice and wearing an expensive leather jacket and nice shoes and a gold ring and a thick gold chain on his wrist. He had booked her for two hours incall and as soon as she let her in he had given her the money, £300 in an envelope. She had put the money in a kitchen drawer which is where she keeps all her money. Then she had given him a drink and they had sex on the sofa in the sitting room and then they went into the bedroom and they had sex again. Dao said that he was quite funny and made her laugh. After they had sex for the second time she went into the bathroom to shower. When she came out he had already got dressed and he seemed in a hurry to go. He told her that he had a meeting and he went. It was only when Dao's second customer came that she realised that Ronnie had taken all the money that was in the drawer. Yes, he had taken the £300 he had brought but she also had another £2,400 in the drawer and he had taken that as well. She was so upset that she gave the second customer his money back and told him to go because she was too upset to work.

Oliver said it was her own fault and that she still had to pay him the £100 commission from Ronnie and the commission from the second customer, even though she hadn't had sex with him. Dao said that it wasn't fair but I could understand why Oliver wanted his money because really it wasn't his fault. I felt very sorry for Dao but really it was her own fault for leaving all her money in the kitchen and for letting the customer see where she kept her money. I know that stealing is wrong but that doesn't mean that people don't steal. People do steal so you have to be careful with your money.

I never let a customer see where I hide my money. In fact I never hide my money while a customer is there. When the customer gives me my money I say thank you and give them a kiss on the cheek and then I put the money on the coffee table. That is when I phone Oliver to say that everything is okay. But then I leave the money on the coffee table so that I can see where it is. Then if the customer tries to take the money I will see what he is doing straight away. Then when he has gone I hide it in the kitchen drawer where I keep my book. Then when I have a thousand pounds in the drawer I put it in an envelope and hide it under the carpet behind the sofa. Do you know I have more than £25,000 now? In Thailand you would have to work for more than four years to earn that much money and I have it in cash under my carpet. All the girls are careful where they hide their money. Nancy puts it behind a panel under the bath and Sandra keeps it in the freezer compartment of her fridge. I don't know where Alice keeps hers because she won't say.

I explained to Dao about hiding her money and she listened and said that I was very clever at this job. Actually, she is right. I have only been doing this job for three months but I do know many things. I think now I am quite professional.

Dao kept crying and saying that Oliver wasn't fair. Ronnie had stolen £2,700 from her and £900 of that money was for Oliver. So she had lost £2,700 but she had to give Oliver £900 so really she had lost £3,600. And she had to give him £50 for the customer she had sent away. Dao said it was Oliver's fault because Oliver had sent her the customer. He had sent her the man who had stolen from her so he was to blame, not her. I didn't want to argue with her but really I thought that it was her fault, not Oliver's.

Dao said that Oliver should check on the customers, but he can't really do that. Oliver never gets to meet them, he only talks to them on the phone. Oliver told Dao that he had called Ronnie's number but the phone had been switched off. I think he probably threw the SIM card away. Dao started crying again and asked me what she should do. I said there was nothing she could do. She couldn't go to the police so she would just have to work hard to make more money. She started crying again and said that she owed money to Cat and to Oliver and she had to pay her council tax and her electricity bill and she needed more condoms and shampoo. I said that I would lend her £1,000 and she stopped crying and hugged me and said that I was a good friend. Then Oliver rang me and said that I had a two hour booking so I had to go back home.

My customer was called Tim and he was an estate agent, tall and quite good-looking. Everything was okay until he asked me if I would do anal, and I said I wouldn't. Some of the girls do but I never have. I think it would hurt too much. Tim said he would pay me an extra £50 if I did anal with him but I said that it wasn't about money, it was about not wanting to do it. I told him that I wasn't a trisexual, and he said that he didn't understand. I said I wouldn't try everything sexual and he laughed and then it was all okay. He asked me for my number when he left and I gave it to him because actually he was a good customer.

Simon came with a pizza and we ate it and watched a Netflix movie. When the movie was finished we had sex in the bedroom and then I gave him a massage. Simon said that if I married him and stopped doing this job he would buy me a house in Thailand and take care of me for ever. I said I was happy to take care of myself but that he was my favourite customer and that made him a little bit happy.

Chapter 47

Friday May 29. I thought a lot about Dao and the money she lost. I think I am stupid to keep all my money in the flat, but I am not sure what to do with it. I have an account with the Kasikorn Bank in Udon Thani. Kasikorn means Thai Farmer. Actually the bank used to be called Thai Farmers Bank but the owners of the bank thought that the name confused farangs so they changed it but now I think farangs are even more confused because they don't know what Kasikorn means. The problem is I do not know how to get the cash from my room into my bank account in Udon Thani. I was going to ask Kung to help me but now I know that he is only using me so I can not ask him. I think the best way is to send it to my mother so that she can put it into my bank account. I think what I will do is to put fifty pound notes into a DVD case and send it to my mother. I can get £2,000 into one case so I will put two cases into a padded envelope and send it to my mother. She can then put the £4,000 into my bank account and they will change it into Thai baht for me. I think it is a good plan.

Yesterday I had three customers. One was a young man in a suit who was so nervous that he kept stammering. He was quite cute. I think it might have been his first time with a working girl because he didn't know what to do. And he came so quickly that he was very embarrassed. He said that he had always wanted to try an Asian girl and I said it was okay, we were the same as any other girl. After he came I gave him a massage and then oral and he got hard again and the second time was much better. Afterwards he said that actually it was his first time with a girl, that he was a virgin before he came to see me, but I am not sure if he is telling the truth or not. His name was Phillip and I gave him my phone number.

The second customer was called Jon, without an 'H'. I actually have three customers called Jon without an 'H'. They are all English. The Jon from yesterday was very tall and thin, he looked like he could be a basketball player. He had to bend his head when he walked into my bedroom so that he wouldn't bang it on the door and his feet were hanging over the edge of the bed. He looked like a giant. Jon said he worked for a double glazing company and that he had just been paid a big bonus so he wanted to treat himself. I thought that was quite sweet, it was like I was a prize. I couldn't give him a bubble bath because he was too tall but I showered with him and then we had sex in the bedroom, with me on top. It was funny seeing his feet sticking off the edge of the bed but I tried not to laugh. I think he is my tallest customer by far.

The third customer was called Mark. Mark booked me for two hours and he said he drove a delivery van but I don't think he was telling the truth. Actually he reminded me of Vince and I think maybe he sold drugs. But I don't care if customers lie to me or not, all I care about is if they are good customers and Mark was okay. He wanted oral and then sex doggy-style while he watched me in the mirror. I did what I always do when I do it that way and look at his eyes in the mirror and open my mouth a bit and lick my lips, the way that Candy showed me. And I moan a bit and say 'yes, yes, yes' because customers like to think that I'm enjoying it. I'm not sure why that is, because they are paying me for sex so why does it matter whether I like it or not? All that should matter is how it feels, right? But I've noticed that if I pretend to come when the customer is having sex with me, they come at the same time or very soon afterwards. It's as if seeing me come makes it more sexier for them. Now I always pretend to come. Actually, sometimes I really do come, but not often. And I don't think a customer can tell the difference. That is the big difference between a man and a woman, I think. With a man, you always know if he comes. There is evidence. But with a woman, you never really can tell.

Chapter 48

Saturday May 30. I went to the Post Office yesterday and I sent the envelope to my mum in Udon Thani. I had to queue outside and wear a mask before I went in. Everyone was standing six feet apart and nobody looked happy. I sent the envelope by Registered Post so that she will have to sign for it when she gets it so I know that it will get there safely. I put in a letter telling her to take it right to the bank and not to give any of it to Kung, even if he asks. Sometimes Kung goes to my mum's house to see her and Ice and I don't want her giving him any of my money.

I spoke to Kung yesterday. He phoned me six times and I didn't answer, but then I answered the seventh time. It was two o'clock in the morning so I told him that I had just got home from the restaurant. He didn't ask me how I was or anything, he just started talking about the house immediately. He said he wanted to put a 46 inch plasma television in the bedroom but that he would need 60,000 baht for that which is almost £1,000. And he said the builder wanted another 35,000 baht for the marble tiles in the master bathroom. And he said he might be able to buy another piece of land at the back of the house so that we could make the garden bigger. The land would cost 100,000 baht and another 50,000 baht to build a wall around it. He wanted to know when I could send him the money because he didn't want someone else to buy the land.

Can you believe it? He was asking me for 245,000 baht which is more than £6,000 but I am supposed to be working as a waitress in a Thai restaurant. I knew then for sure one hundred per cent that he is using me, He knows that I am working for the agency, he knows that I am selling my body. He knows and he doesn't care. All he cares about is the money that I send him.

I didn't say anything, though. I just said I didn't have much money but I would try to get some. That was a lie. I am lying to him now the same way that he lies to me. I will lie to him while I work out what I can do.

Vince came to see me in the afternoon. He phoned Oliver and booked me under his real name. I think he forgot that he used to be James. Actually, I thought that Oliver should have realised because he should be keeping a record of who comes to see me, for security. But I think Oliver isn't worried about security, he is just worried about the commission I am to pay him. Anyway, Vince booked me for two hours and he was very happy because he had just sold some cocaine to a group of students and they had spent £2,000.

I gave him a bubble bath and oral and then we had sex. I didn't come but I pretended to. Afterwards I asked him about his money. I said that I didn't know what to do with mine and I wanted to send some to my bank in Thailand. Vince said you had to be careful when you put money in the bank in England because sometimes the banks would tell the police about you. He said if the police found out you were putting a lot of cash in the bank then they would ask you where it came from and if it was illegal then they would take it off you.

I asked him what he did with his money and he laughed and said that he used Smurfs. I didn't know what a Smurf was. He explained that a Smurf was someone who put money into the bank for you. You paid them to put small amounts of money into lots of bank accounts. Instead of putting £10,000 into one bank you put £1,000 into each of ten banks. And you paid the Smurfs a commission of five per cent. For every one thousand pounds they paid in, you gave them £50. You had to trust the Smurfs, of course, because they might run away with your money. If they did that you had to find the Smurf and hurt him to show to the other Smurfs that it was not a good idea to steal. Vince said that most of his Smurfs were students. He said if I wanted I could use his Smurfs. He said what I should do is to open a bank account using my passport and my electricity bill or something else that showed where I lived, and I should deposit about £500. Then I should give money to Smurfs and they will pay it into different accounts and then transfer it my account. Because it is small amounts of money, the police don't care. Vince says that every week he gives more than £10,000 to the Smurfs. Then he transfers the money to banks in Jersey and Hungary and he said that even if the police catch him they will never get his money. I think Vince is quite clever so I said okay, I would like to use his Smurfs. I didn't want him to see where I hide my money but I did have £800 in my kitchen drawer plus the £300 he had paid me so I asked him if I could give him the £1,100 to give to the Smurfs. He laughed and said that I had to open my bank account first. Then he said he had a better idea, he said I could give him the £1,100 and he would transfer £1,100 from his account to my account in Thailand. That seemed like a great idea to me so I gave him the money and the number of my bank account in Udon Thani. I am so glad to have met Vince.

Chapter 49

Sunday May 31. Yesterday Nancy called me and asked me if I wanted to go to her apartment to watch Thai soap operas on the internet. I said I had to clean my flat. The real reason that I didn't want to go to Nancy's flat was because I didn't want to see Chris. He keeps sending me text messages asking if he can come to my flat to see me but I ignore him. It is not fair. He is Nancy's boyfriend so he should not be trying to have sex with me. I think I should tell Nancy but I am scared that if I do she will blame me.

In the evening I had a customer at six o'clock. His name was Richard and he came in a tracksuit and running shoes. He said he lived in Queensway which is not too far away and that he had told his wife that he had gone out running. People are allowed out once a day to exercise. It was so funny. We had sex, twice, and then he put his tracksuit back on and went. He didn't want to shower because he wanted to go back all sweaty so that his wife would believe he had been out running. I wonder what she would think if she found out what had really made him sweat! He was going for sexercise, not exercise!

Then Bee phoned me and asked if she could come to my flat because she wanted to talk to me. I had an outcall booking at eleven o'clock but said that she could come and see me before then so she came at eight o'clock. She brought a whole watermelon with her which was nice because she remembered how much I like to eat watermelon. I made her some Japanese green tea and we drank it and ate the watermelon.

Bee said that she was really busy which was why she wanted to talk to me. She said that some days she was having to turn down customers and she was worried that she might lose business if those customers started going somewhere else. She wanted to send some customers to see me on the days when she was busy. Her customers paid £200 an hour and she said that I could keep £160 and just give her £40. Actually that is a very good deal. When I see a customer through

Oliver's agency I charge £150 an hour but I only get to keep £100 for myself. If I saw Bee's customers I would keep £160. That is a big difference. Bee said that if I wanted I could put my photographs on her website. That way some customers might ask to see me and she would do the same deal and let me keep £160.

I think it would be great to have the extra money but I don't think Oliver would be happy. That is what I said to Bee but she said that Oliver wouldn't know and I said well of course he would if he saw my photographs and she said that the photographer could hide my face or blur it a bit.

I said that I didn't think it would be fair to Oliver and she said that Oliver wasn't fair to his girls, that he took a third of what they earned and all he did was answer the phone. Actually there is more to it than that but I didn't want to argue with Bee. I said I would think about it but really I have already made up my mind.

Then Bee started asking questions about Alice and I realised that she is still angry about the fight at the Sloane Square flat. The bruise on her face doesn't look too bad now and with her make up on you can hardly see it, but I don't think she has forgotten or forgiven Alice. Then Bee told me a story about Alice that I am not sure is true or not. She said that Alice used to be a go-go dancer in Soi Cowboy in a bar called Long Gun. She said that Alice took a lot of drugs, especially a drug called Yar Bar. A lot of go-go dancers take Yar Bar, she said, because it gives them energy, but it also makes them crazy. That is why it is called Yar Bar. In Thai that means Crazy Drug.

Bee said that Alice was always fighting with girls in other bars in Soi Cowboy, because she was jealous if they went with her customers. And one night she got into a fight with another dancer and hit her with a bottle, the same as she hit Bee. But the bottle broke and the glass cut the other girl's throat and she died. The police came but Alice ran away and she got a passport in the name of another girl and she came to England. Bee said that Alice can't go back to Thailand because the police are still looking for her, and if they knew that she was in London they would come to get her. I don't know if that story is true and Bee wouldn't say how she knew.

I asked her about the magic perfume that makes men fall in love and she said that if I wanted I could use it one day. It definitely worked, she said, which is why it is so expensive. She had used it on four customers now and they all wanted to marry her and take care of her. She said she was careful who she used it on because she didn't want someone ugly or poor falling in love with her. The best thing was for someone rich and old because then they would die soon and she would get all their money. She might marry the rich American customer she had, but first he had to build her a house and give her a car to prove that he did have money. If he did that then she might marry him. He was quite old and she thought that he might die soon. She smiled and said that if he didn't die soon then she had another magic potion that would take care of that and then she laughed but I don't think she was joking. I think she was serious. I know that Alice is dangerous but actually I think Bee is dangerous, too.

Chapter 50

Monday June 1. I have been an escort for three months now. I know I am a very different girl from when I started doing this job. For a start, I never cry any more. There is nothing to cry about. I make love for money, that is my job. And the better I do my job, the more money I get. I get to live in a nice apartment and I wear nice clothes and I can eat good food and do whatever I want. I am happy, I think. I try not to think about how many men I have had sex with. It is a lot. I could go to my book and count but really I do not want to.

Yesterday evening Nancy and Sandra came to my flat to pay me back some of the money that they owed me. Nancy paid me back £500 and Sandra paid me back £1,000. Sandra said she had had a really good week and they both thanked me, which was nice.

Sandra said that Bee still hadn't paid her back any of the money she had borrowed and I said that maybe she should ask her again because now she was very busy. Sandra asked me how I knew and I said that she had come to see me, and I told them about Bee asking me to take care of some of her customers. I told them I wasn't going to do it, of course, because it wouldn't be fair to Oliver. Sandra seemed really angry and said that it wasn't fair, that if Bee was earning good money then she should pay her back straight away.

I told them what Bee had said about Alice, but said that it was a secret and that nobody should tell Alice. Sandra said that she knew that Alice used to be a dancer in Soi Cowboy but she didn't know if she had ever killed anybody.

Nancy said that she had something to tell us. She has a friend who works for the A1 agency, which is one of the biggest in London, and she said that one of the A1 girls had been robbed. Not robbed like Dao had been robbed, but tied up and beaten until she told the robber where she kept her money. Now she was in hospital. I asked Nancy if the girl had spoken to the police but Nancy said she couldn't because she was in England illegally. She had come over using another girl's passport and that passport had been sent back to Thailand. So she had no passport and no visa and if the police caught her they would send her back to Thailand straight away. And Nancy said that even if the girl went to the police there was no evidence like CCTV pictures because the flat she worked in didn't have CCTV. I felt very sorry for the girl, but she should have had a flat with CCTV really. I asked Nancy if the policeman I had met, the one called Neil, had talked to the A1 girls and she said that he had but because the girl didn't have CCTV she couldn't see who the customer was before she opened the door. That is not a good idea. A working girl should always know who is outside the door before she opens it.

We had arranged to eat at Cat's flat so we shared an Uber taxi to Sloane Square. Cat was cooking Pad Thai and Thod Mun Pla which she cooks really well, and she had brought some red pork from Chinatown and I had brought some lychees that I had bought from a shop in Edgware Road. All the rest of the girls were already in the flat and Alice and Rachel were already a little drunk, I think. They seem to be best friends, they always laugh at each other's jokes and they kept clinking their glasses together.

We ate the food and then we played cards. Rachel and Alice were drinking a lot, and everybody seemed happy. Then Alice and Sandra got into a bit of an argument, over nothing really. I think Alice wanted more ice and she asked Sandra to get it from the fridge and Sandra said she wasn't a maid and Alice told her not to be stupid because she was dealing the cards so she couldn't go to the kitchen and then Sandra said what would Alice do, kill her like she killed the girl in Soi Cowboy. I think she only said it because she was a bit drunk and she was joking, but Alice got really angry and asked her what she meant and then Sandra said that Bee had told me the story of what had happened in Soi Cowboy and then everybody was looking at me and I just wanted to cry. Oliver was angry at me because I had been talking to Bee, Alice was angry at me because she thought I had been telling lies about her, and I was angry at Sandra for getting me into trouble. Alice started shouting and I thought that she was going to hit me with a bottle but Rachel calmed her down and Dao took me into one of the bedrooms because she could see how upset I was.

Oliver and Cat calmed everyone down and Dao and I went back into the main room and played cards again but I could tell that Alice still wasn't happy. But she said that it wasn't me that she was angry at, it was Bee. She wanted to kill Bee, she said, and I think that she means it. I just kept quiet and played cards. I lost a lot of money. More than £1,000.

When we had finished I went home with Dao because I didn't want to sleep alone. She told me not to worry and that it was just because Alice was drunk. I like Dao. She really does care about people. But she didn't talk about the money she owes me. I told her about the girl at A1 who had been beaten up and told her that she was lucky that she wasn't hurt when she was robbed and she agreed with me. Money is just money, we can always earn more money if we have to.

Chapter 51

Wednesday June 3. Yesterday I worked with Dao for the first time. The customer called Patrick from Belfast who I had seen with Nancy wanted to see me and Dao so he booked us for two hours incall at my apartment.

Dao came to my apartment first and she said she was a bit nervous because it was the first time she had worked with another girl. I said there was nothing to worry about because it was actually easy but she said that she wanted a drink so she opened a bottle of wine and drank two glasses before Patrick came. She was wearing black suspenders and a black bra so I put on my red suspenders and my black vinyl thigh-length boots which I think make me look very sexy. Patrick came at six o'clock and paid me and Dao straight away with £300 each. He had brought a bottle of champagne with him which was nice, so I went to the kitchen to open it. When I came back Dao was already giving him oral on the sofa so I took off my bra and started kissing him. Dao didn't seem shy at all. Patrick asked her to kiss me, and she did, and then he asked us for a lesbian show so I licked and kissed her and she moaned as if she was really enjoying it.

After we had sex Patrick had a shower and then he came back to the bedroom and we gave him a body massage using lots of oil. I asked him why he hadn't booked me and Nancy and he said that he had seen the photographs of me and Dao on the website and thought that we looked very sexy. He said that maybe next time he might book me, Dao and Nancy together. Can you believe that? One man and three girls? Actually I think that might be fun.

After Patrick and Dao had gone I phoned my mother in Thailand and asked her about the envelope but it hadn't arrived yet. Then I spoke to Ice and he kept asking me when I was coming home and I said I didn't know, that I was working hard to make a better life for him and me but that I loved him and missed him so much. That is true,

I miss him every hour of every day. But I have to make money so I have to do this job.

Chapter 52

Friday June 5. I think Kung is a really bad person. My mother says it is wrong to hate anybody but Kung has been so bad that I am starting to hate him. On Wednesday evening he phoned me again and asked me to send him money so that he could buy the land behind the house. He said if I didn't send it right away someone else might buy the land and build a factory next to our house and that would be terrible. He asked if I could send him 245,000 baht. He could only ask for all that money because he knows that I am selling my body in London. If he believed I was working in a restaurant then he would know that I can not earn so much.

I asked him if he really loved me and he said yes. Then I asked if he would leave his wife and live with me and Ice and he said that was difficult because he did not want to hurt his family. I said that was not fair because he was hurting my family and he said that I had to understand him. Then he asked me to call him back because it was expensive to phone me from Thailand. Can you believe that? I called him back and this time I was angry but very cold. *Jai Yen*, we say in Thai. Cool heart. I said that I thought it might be better if I had the house myself. That way he wouldn't have to come and live with me and Ice and I could take care of myself. I asked him how much I would have to pay him to have the house to myself, and do you know what he said? He said two million baht. I know that is not fair because the house is worth three million baht. I said that one and a half million baht would be fair and he said it wasn't fair because he had been doing all the work, talking to the builders and the bank and organising everything. I felt like I wanted to cry because I had given him so much of my life. I was waiting for him to leave his wife but now I know that he never will.

Thursday was a very busy day. I did two hours incall with Nancy in her apartment with an American lawyer called Hank. Nancy didn't say anything about paying me back the money she owed me, which annoyed me a lot because Hank gave her £420 plus a $100 tip.

Then I had one customer who was French. His name was Alain and he was bald and a bit fat but very nice. He had booked me for two hours incall and he asked me if I knew where he could get some cocaine so I phoned Vince and he came around with some. Alain asked me if I wanted some and actually I was a bit tired so I did sniff a bit, just to get some energy. Actually, it felt quite good, but I do not want to take it too often.

After Alain left Oliver phoned to say that Simon had booked me for three hours incall which was great because Simon always wants to watch a Netflix movie and eat with me. He only has sex once so it's easy work and he is quite nice, even though he keeps asking me to stop work and to live with him, which is a bit annoying.

Chapter 53

Sunday June 7. Yesterday I worked with Candy for the first time. It doesn't say on the website that I will work with Candy, but Oliver phoned me and asked me if I would do it because a customer wanted something special. He wanted domination with two girls and he had seen my picture and wanted me to do it with Candy. I said I didn't want to be dominated but he said no, it would be me and Candy dominating him. He wanted to book us for two hours incall and because we would be doing domination he would be paying extra – he would pay us each £420, the same price as outcall. I said okay because actually I wanted to see what domination was like.

The customer had booked us for seven o'clock but Oliver said I should get to Candy's apartment at six o'clock so that she could show me what to do. Candy has a two-bedroom apartment near to Paddington station in an old building but it has CCTV which is good. She pays £550 a week which is quite expensive but she said she needed two bedrooms because she does domination. She showed me the second bedroom and I was so surprised. For a start she had covered all the walls and the window with black plastic from garbage bags and there were red candles everywhere. There was no bed in the room but a sort of table covered with black leather and there was a cage made of black metal bars that was just big enough for a man and a thing made of wood that had holes for a man's neck and his wrists with locks so that he couldn't get out. Hanging on the walls were whips and paddles and straps that Candy said she used to hit the customer with, and lots of other things like little balls on strings and metal clamps and dildoes, some of them really big.

I asked her how she knew what to do to the customer and she said that when the customer first came she sat down with them and asked them everything that they liked to do and everything they didn't like to do. The customer she was seeing was one she had seen before so she knew what to do.

She said that she always gave the customer what she calls a safe word. For this customer the safe word is 'high heels' though actually that is two words. If the customer says the safe word then we have to stop straight away. But if he says anything else like 'stop' or 'no' or if he screams, we carry on doing it because really he does not want us to stop. It sounds a bit crazy but Candy said it is very important because we don't keep stopping just because we think we are hurting him too much. Unless he says the safe word, we are not hurting him too much.

Candy said most customers who want domination do not want sex, not even oral, but that they often made themselves come. Or sometimes they did not want to come at all. She showed me her outfits. She has a lot of domination outfits and masks and things, most of them made from plastic or leather. She gave me a very short leather skirt and a leather jacket with chains on it and high-heeled boots. She wore fishnet stockings and a leather bra and a leather g-string with chrome studs on it.

The customer's name was Luke. He was about forty years old and quite short and not very handsome and it was very funny what we had to do to him. Candy told him to take his clothes off and kneel down and then she spat into a saucer and I did the same and then he licked it up like a dog. Then she made him lick our feet, but it wasn't sexy like when Robert licks my feet, it was like he was a dog. Then she started calling him all sorts of names, telling him he was no good, and then she whipped him with a leather whip.

Then we took him into the bathroom and she told him to lie down in the bath and then she told me to pee on him. Can you believe it? It was quite difficult to pee because I didn't feel like it, but I managed. And do you know what? He drank some of my pee. I don't know why anyone would want to do that but he did. We did a lot more things to him which I think were cruel and stupid, but afterwards when he was dressed he thanked us both and gave us both £50 tips so he must have been happy. Men can be so strange sometimes.

On the television news they were talking about a demonstration in Trafalgar Square by a group called Black Lives Matter who want to destroy statues. There are many statues in Trafalgar Square including four huge lions. I do not understand why these people hate statues but there were thousands of them and most of them were not wearing masks. The police were there and we thought the police would send the protestors home but instead the police knelt down in front of them. It was so strange. In Thailand the police only kneel in front of the king and the royal family. They would never kneel in front of a crowd of angry people. I do not understand what happened. The police walk through the parks now telling people not to gather in groups, but when they see thousands of people in Trafalgar Square they kneel down.

Chapter 54

Monday June 8. Sandra and Nancy came around to my flat before we went to Sloane Square in an Uber taxi. Cat cooked Tom Yam Kung which is a hot and spicy prawn soup that was really delicious and Candy had brought some fruit, and Nancy had a bottle of brandy that a customer had given her. I didn't drink any of the brandy but everyone else did and they got a bit drunk.

Wanda said she thought there was a ghost in her flat that was bringing her bad luck which sounds crazy but actually Thai people believe in ghosts. The ghost of my grandfather once gave my mother the winning numbers for the lottery and she won one thousand baht. Wanda said she wanted to talk to the ghost to see what it wanted but she didn't know how to talk to ghosts. In Thailand we call ghosts Pee. Cat said that she did, she had done it before, so she said that one day this week we would go to the flat and try to talk to the ghost. The more people that went the better, she said, because ghosts couldn't do bad things if there were many people there. Alice said that ghosts didn't always want to do bad things, sometimes they wanted to help and I said that was true and told them the story about my grandfather giving the lottery numbers to my mother.

Before we went home, Oliver said that there was something special that we had to do next Saturday. He had a friend who was a Russian who wanted to have a big birthday party at his house and all of us girls would have to go. We would have to go to a house in St John's Wood and there would be other girls there and a lot of the Russian's friends. Nancy asked how much we would charge and Oliver said that actually because the man was a friend of his he wouldn't be paying and everyone said that wasn't fair because we were working girls and we didn't do sex for free. Oliver was a bit angry and said that we didn't understand, the man was a friend so he couldn't charge him but Alice and Rachel said that he had to pay because we would be working. Oliver said that okay, he would pay us. He would give us £300 each and we wouldn't have to pay him any commission. The party would start at ten o'clock at night. Alice wanted to know when the party would finish and Oliver said that he didn't know, but that it would be fun and there would be lots of food and drink and drugs and we would all have a good time. I don't think that he understands that even when we are having a good time we are still working. Wanda asked about Covid and said that really we shouldn't be going into the house together but Oliver just laughed. He said if the police stopped us we could just say we were with Black Lives Matter and they would kneel down. We all laughed at that.

Chapter 55

Wednesday June 10. I phoned my mother about the money I posted her and she said that it hadn't arrived yet. I am starting to think that perhaps I was a bit crazy to post £4,000 to Thailand.

In the afternoon Cat phoned me and said she was going to Wanda's apartment in Queensway with Sandra and Alice and Rachel to talk to ghosts and she asked me if I would go, too. I walked around to Wanda's apartment. It was in quite a nice building and it had CCTV which is important. There was no lift and her apartment was on the third floor and that's not so good because customers don't like to climb stairs. Actually, a lot of girls like basement flats because they have their entrance and customers just have to walk down a few stairs to the door. That way no one can see them come and go. Some customers are shy, you see. Especially the ones who are married.

Cat was already there with Sandra and Wanda and Wanda made coffee for us and then Alice and Rachel arrived. Alice said she couldn't stay long because a regular customer had booked her for four hours outcall so Cat said we should get started right away. Wanda cleared everything off her glass coffee table and Cat wrote down letters on pieces of paper. She wrote down the English alphabet and the numbers one to ten and Wanda asked her why she wasn't using the Thai alphabet and Cat said it was because if there was a Pee in the apartment it would be a farang Pee and not a Thai Pee and a farang Pee would not understand the Thai alphabet.

Cat also wrote down 'YES' and 'NO' and 'DON'T KNOW' then she put those pieces of paper in the middle and surrounded them with the twenty-six letters of the alphabet. In fact I think it is better to use the English alphabet because the Thai alphabet has 44 letters and more than twenty vowels. Cat told Wanda to light candles and close the curtains and she did and we sat around the table and Cat put a glass on the table upside down and said we should all touch it with the fingers of our left hands. Actually I have done this before in Thailand with my friends when we were at school and I always think that somebody is pushing the glass and that really it is just for fun and not for talking to Pee but Cat was very serious.

Cat said the Lord's Prayer which is the prayer that Christians say, which I thought was strange because we are all Buddhists but Cat said it was because the ghost would most likely be a farang. Then she asked if any spirits were there. She spoke in English. Then the glass slid towards 'YES', quite slowly. Cat asked for the name of the Pee and the glass spelled out 'J-U-L-I-E'. It was a bit scary actually because I don't think anyone was pushing the glass. Julie is a girl's name. Cat asked Julie how old she was and the glass went to the number 10 and then the number 2 and when Cat asked if that meant that Julie was 12 the glass moved to 'YES'. Cat asked Julie where she was and the glass moved really quickly to 'DON'T KNOW' and then it slowly spelled out 'D-A-R-K' which was a bit scary. Wanda looked a bit worried but Alice and Rachel kept joking until Cat scolded them and told them to take it seriously or they would upset the Pee.

Then Cat asked the Pee if she had a message for anyone and the glass went to 'YES'. Cat asked what the message was and the glass stopped for a minute or two as if it was thinking and then it slowly spelled out 'D-A-N-G-R-E' which didn't make sense and then Sandra said maybe it meant DANGER.

Cat asked who the message was for and the glass stayed still. She asked again and said 'Please Julie tell us who the message is for' and the glass started to move. It spelled out 'E-V-R-Y-B-D-Y' which I think means it was trying to spell EVERYBODY.

Then Wanda's phone rang and made us all jump! It was Oliver phoning to say that she had an incall customer who was coming in fifteen minutes so we all had to go. Actually I am glad that he phoned then because I did not like talking to Julie. I believe in Pee and I believe that sometimes Pee want to talk to people.

Chapter 56

Thursday June 11. Yesterday a customer booked me and Nancy together for two hours incall in the afternoon. I went around to Nancy's apartment and we changed into sexy dresses and high heels and put on sexy makeup. His name was Alex and he was about fifty years old and wearing a suit. I think he had taken Viagra because he was red faced and he kept sniffing and he made love to me three times and four times with Nancy. He kept changing from me to her which meant that we had to use lots of condoms. Then after he came he asked if we would do a lesbian show for him so we did. Then we gave him a massage and he was still hard and he said that he wanted to do anal and I said that I wouldn't. Nancy said that she wouldn't either but then Alex said that he would pay an extra £50 so Nancy said that she would. After he had gone away Nancy said that actually anal was quite nice and she didn't mind doing it with her boyfriend but she always made customers pay extra for it. I don't think she tells Oliver that she is getting extra money from customers but that is not my business.

I was glad that Chris was not in the flat because I am still angry at him for coming around to my flat and he still sends me texts saying that he wants me to be his girlfriend. I think he is crazy because Nancy really likes him a lot and gives him FFF and money too.

Then I remembered that this was the time of the month that Nancy had her period and I asked her how she could work and she said that her period hadn't come yet. She laughed and said that she hoped she wasn't pregnant but I don't think it is anything to laugh at. If she is pregnant she can not work. She said that maybe the famous customer had made her pregnant so she would get money from him for the rest of her life. Actually I think that sometimes Nancy is a bit crazy.

I told her about talking with the Pee with Cat at Wanda's flat and she said that we should buy Julie something to make her happy. If you gave a present to a ghost then it would not be so angry. It sounded like a good idea so we went to a corner shop that was still open. Nancy bought some chocolates because all young girls like chocolates and I looked for a doll so that she would have something to play with. Do you know what I found? I found a doll called Julie. It was in a box with pretty clothes and a toy dog so I bought it because I thought that Julie would be happy to have a doll that had her name.

Nancy and I went to Wanda's apartment and we gave the presents to her and she put them on top of her wardrobe where she keeps her Buddha figure and her candles. She said it was a very good idea to give Julie presents. I asked her if she thought that Julie was happy or not and Wanda said she thought that she wasn't because sometimes the room felt cold even when it was warm and sometimes Wanda felt sad even though nothing was wrong. She said that she wanted Cat to come back some time to talk to Julie again and Nancy said she would come because she wanted to ask Julie for numbers to play the English lottery because with the English lottery you can win millions of pounds which is a lot more than you can win in Thailand.

Wanda cooked some Phad Thai for us and we ate it in the kitchen. Wanda told us about her life before she came to London. She was born in Buri Ram and has a five-year-old daughter who lives with her mother. Her husband was a bus driver but he left her when her daughter was born and she discovered that he had three different wives all over Thailand. Wanda had a job in a factory but the work was very hard so she went to be a working girl in Singapore. A friend told her how to do it and she said it was easy money. Thai people need visas to go to most countries, but not to Singapore. Thai people can get a two week visa on arrival and sometimes a month. So Wanda went to Singapore with her friend who was quite pretty and they shared a room in a hotel and in the evenings they went to a building called Orchard Towers. Wanda said that farangs called it the 'Four Floors of Horse' which I didn't understand but then she spelled it out for me and I realised that she meant 'Four Floors of Whores.' Her English isn't very good, actually. In the building there are lots of bars and Thai girls can find customers there. There are a lot of ladyboys working there too, and Filipina girls too. Wanda said a farang will pay 300 Singapore dollars to go with a girl which is about £100 and so it is almost as much as we get working in London. Wanda said that she could get two or three customers a night which was really good money. She had to leave every two weeks but the ticket to Singapore only cost about

10,000 baht and the room she stayed in was quite cheap. Just working for two weeks she could save about 100,000 baht. She would work for two weeks and then fly back to Thailand for two weeks.

She did that for six months but she wanted to earn more money so that she could build her own house in Buri Ram so she used the money she had saved to buy a contract to get a visa to work in London. Now she has already built her house. Now she is saving her money so that she can set up a restaurant in Buri Ram and when she has enough she will stop doing this job and go back to Thailand.

Wanda is very sensible. She says she will never have a boyfriend until she is back in Thailand and she never takes drugs. She is also careful when she plays cards at the Sloane Square flat. She says you have to be very careful with your money in this job. It is easy to earn it, but it is easy to lose it, too. Wanda talks a lot of sense. She is more sensible than Nancy who is wasting all her money on her boyfriend.

Then Oliver phoned me to say that Robert had booked me for four hours so I had to go home to change into my school uniform. As I was leaving the apartment, Simon phoned me to say that he had tried to book me but the agency had said that I was busy. I said that was true and he asked me if I would cancel my customer so that he could see me but I said that I was sorry but that was impossible. I have to go with the customer who books me first. Simon complained and said that he wanted to be my boyfriend and not my customer and I said that I was sorry but I had to go. I don't like it when he says he wants to be my boyfriend. He is my customer and that is the end of it.

Chapter 57

Friday June 12. I phoned my mum she told me that the £4,000 I had sent had arrived, which was good news. Then she said that she had already changed the pounds into Thai baht but had spent a lot of it. I asked her what she had spent it on and she said that she had to go tamboon at the wat. The wat is the temple and to go tamboon means to make merit and she had give the monks thirty thousand baht which is more than £400. And she said that one of her friends needed money because her daughter was in hospital so she had loaned her forty thousand baht. And the airconditioner in her bedroom wasn't working so she had bought a new one and that had cost thirty-five thousand baht. She said that my father wanted a new motorcycle too and that was going to cost twenty-five thousand baht. I started to cry because this wasn't fair. Everybody is taking money from me. I have to work so hard to make my money and I don't think they understand just how hard I work. My mother has spent about half the money I sent. That is not fair because it wasn't her money it was my money. I didn't tell her how upset I was and I don't think she realises that she has done something wrong. In a way I think my mother is a bit like Kung. She cares more about my money than she does about me.

Even though I was very unhappy I still had to work. I had four customers yesterday. The first customer was Matt, the man with his name tattooed in Thai on his arm and the tattoo of a Buddha's head. He said that he had just got back from Thailand and that he had had sex with twenty girls in two weeks. He had been in Pattaya most of the time and he said all the girls in Pattaya liked sex. I think he believes that girls like having sex with him but in fact they are only doing it for money. I don't think any girl would enjoy having sex with Matt. He is rude and ugly and he doesn't smell good. He kept trying to talk to me in really bad Thai but I said that I didn't speak Thai. When he left he asked me for my phone number again and I said no. After he left I phoned Oliver and said that I didn't want to see Matt again. I said he was a bad customer but I didn't say why.

The second customer was called Russ and he was a nice man, quite sweet actually. He was about fifty years old and very polite and kept saying 'please' and 'thank you'. He didn't want sex, just oral, and he wanted me to use a condom even though I would have done it without one.

After Russ had gone I didn't have a customer for three hours and I just lay on my sofa and cried because I was so sad. Then Oliver phoned and said that I had a booking for midnight. It was a new customer called Frankie and he wanted me to wear my nurse's uniform. Frankie was younger than me, I think, and quite handsome. He had a good body but he didn't want sex with me, he just wanted to lie on the bed while I stroked him. He said that when he was small he was in hospital for a long time and he almost died and that now that he was older he liked to pretend that nurses were touching him. I felt a bit sad for him. He said that he didn't have a girlfriend and I gave him my phone number.

After he went I lay on the sofa and cried. I wanted to talk to somebody about my problem but there was no one I could talk to. I felt so alone. I missed Ice and I wanted to see him and hear his voice but I didn't want him to know how upset I was so I didn't talk to him. I miss my son and I wish that I was in Thailand with him now but first I have to sort out my problem. I feel so alone. After midnight I started getting text messages from customers saying good night. I didn't send any replies. I was too sad.

Chapter 58

Sunday June 14. Yesterday was the party in St John's Wood and I didn't get up until very late today. I feel a bit sick and I have a bad headache and I am aching and sore all over. What happened at the party was not good.

Oliver said we were all to meet first at the Sloane Square flat and that we should dress very sexily, the way that we dress for the photographs on the website. I wore my tight black dress and my thigh-length boots, though obviously I had my Kenzo coat on when I went outside. I went to Sloane Square with Nancy in an Uber taxi and Alice and Rachel were already there. Cat had made some Khao Pad for us and we ate it. Oliver said it was very important that everyone at the party was happy. Alice asked when we would get paid and Oliver said that he would sort out the money on Sunday. Rachel wanted to know what we were supposed to do at the party but all Oliver said was that we should make sure that everyone was happy. That's all that he would say. When all the girls arrived Oliver said that we should go.

I went to St John's Wood in a taxi with Oliver and Nancy. Oliver looked a bit nervous and I could tell that he was worried. I had never seen him like that before. Normally he always looks confident but not yesterday. The house we went to was really big. There was a big wall around it and huge iron gates and through the gates we could see lots of cars. There was a red Ferrari and two Porsches and a Range Rover and three BMWs. Oliver had to press a bell and he looked up at a CCTC camera and then the gate opened and we walked in. As we got to the front door two more taxis arrived with Cat, Alice, Sandra, Dao, Rachel, Wanda and Candy so we all went into the house together. There were two men who looked like bodyguards at the front door and Nancy whispered in Thai that she had seen a gun but I didn't see a gun so she might have imagined it.

A big Russian man in a black suit came to say hello to Oliver and hugged him. Oliver said the man was called Nikolai and it was his birthday. Nikolai was fat with his head shaved like a monk and a scar on one of his cheeks. He had really cold blue eyes and he didn't smile. He looked at us like he was a farmer and we were his cows. He said something to Oliver in Russian and Oliver told us to take off our coats. Cat took our coats and Nikolai looked at us and nodded and then pointed to the main room and we all went through. As we went in I saw Oliver give Nikolai a thick envelope which looked like it had a lot of money in it. Nikolai just grunted and put the envelope in his jacket pocket.

There were about forty people in the room, I think. The men were all big and wearing expensive suits and gold chains and they were drinking brandy and whisky and smoking big cigars and shouting at each other in Russian. The women were all tall and pretty and had big breasts and long, long legs. There were blondes and brunettes and redheads and they were all young and pretty and wearing really nice dresses. They were dressed sexily, but not like we were dressed. We Thai girls were dressed like working girls. We were sexy but not sexy like the Russian girls, and I felt a bit shy. Everyone in the room turned to look at us and I know that if I had been there on my own I would have been a bit scared. Some customers look at me like I am a human being, someone they want to talk to and get to know. But some customers look at me like I am an animal, something to be used. I am serious when I say that everyone in the room, the men and the girls, were looking at us as if we were animals. One of the men said something in Russian and they all laughed. I looked at Oliver and he was smiling but I could see that he was a bit nervous.

There was loud music playing on a stereo and there were bottles of spirits everywhere and there were silver bowls with white powder that I knew must be cocaine. But I have never seen so much cocaine in my life. It was like piles of sugar. One of the Russian women was kneeling by a coffee table using a rolled-up fifty pound note to sniff up cocaine. Dao knelt down next to her and the girl gave her the note and Dao sniffed up a lot of cocaine. I mean a lot of cocaine.

Then the girl smiled and she kissed Dao on the lips and I could see that Dao was kissing her back. Oliver said that we should go and talk to the people and do whatever they wanted. I am not sure what he meant but I know that we were working so I smiled and me and Nancy walked over to two men who were standing by a huge TV, the biggest

I have ever seen. It was showing a sexy movie of two blonde girls kissing each other.

The two men said that their names were Viktor and Alexei. They were both quite young, maybe twenty-five, Viktor was wearing an Armani suit and he had a big gold ring with a gold coin in it. He was quite good-looking but like Nikolai he had very hard eyes. He said something to Alexei and they both laughed. Viktor pointed at his groin and said 'Blow Job'. Then he pointed at me. Alexei did the same to Nancy. I couldn't believe it. They wanted oral sex while they were in the room with everyone else. I looked around and Dao was lying on a sofa with the girl who had been sniffing cocaine. The girl was taking off Dao's dress and three men were standing around them, laughing and pointing at them. Alice was kissing a man while Rachel was giving him a blow job and Candy was sitting on the arm of a chair and kissing a man and stroking his leg.

Nancy said we might as well do it because we were there to work so we both knelt down and gave them oral sex. While I was giving Viktor oral a blonde girl came over and she stroked my hair and talked to Viktor. He came in my mouth and then he said he wanted to go upstairs with me and the girl. The girl picked up a bottle of champagne and we went up a big staircase. There were so many bedrooms, more than twelve I am sure. One of the bedroom doors was open and I saw Rachel on top of a man, naked, drinking from a bottle while she made love to him. Two Russian girls were watching Rachel make love and touching themselves and shouting things at her in Russian.

Viktor and the girl took me into another bedroom. Viktor sat on a chair and sniffed some cocaine while the girl started kissing me and undressing me, then she took off her dress and lay on the bed with me. She had a really good body and her skin was so soft and I actually quite enjoyed her stroking and kissing me. Then the girl got off the bed and Viktor told me to give him oral which I did. Then Viktor took off all his clothes and he got on top of me and tried to make love to me and I told him that he had to wear a condom. He said he never wore a condom and he tried to force me but I am quite strong so I pushed him off but then the girl held my arms and shouted at me that I was a whore and I had to do what they wanted and I said that I wasn't a whore but Viktor put his hand over his mouth and then he was inside me and he pushed hard so that it hurt and he kept pounding into me until he came. I wanted to cry. No customer has ever done that to me before. Viktor laughed and rolled off me and I ran into the bathroom to wash out his sperm. I don't want to get sick and I don't want to have a baby. If I am sick or if I get pregnant I cannot work. I spent a lot of time washing myself and when I came out of the bathroom Viktor and the girl had gone so I got dressed.

Alice was in the hallway giving oral sex to a very old man with grey hair. She was naked. She laughed when she saw me and asked me if I was having a good time but I couldn't say anything.

I went downstairs and saw Oliver talking to Nikolai. Nikolai said something to Oliver and Oliver waved me over. Oliver said that Nikolai said that I wasn't smiling and wanted to know what was wrong with me. I told Oliver that the man upstairs had had sex with me without a condom and Oliver asked me if that was a problem. I was so surprised. Of course it is a problem, I said. I never have sex without a condom. Oliver said that it was okay, that all the men there were healthy and no one had Aids. He said something to a girl with long red hair and she went away. Oliver said that I had to relax, that these were his friends and he had to make a good impression. I felt like I wanted to cry because Oliver is my boss and he should understand how I feel.

Then the girl with red hair came back with a glass and Oliver took it and gave it to me and told me to drink it. I said I didn't want to drink alcohol but Oliver said that I had to, it would relax me. I had no choice, I had to drink it. I don't know what it was. Vodka, maybe. With tonic water. Oliver made me drink it all and I was almost sick. Then Cat came over and said in Thai that I had to do whatever Nikolai wanted, that he was a very important man and that if I upset him it would make the agency look bad and give Oliver a big problem. I felt a bit dizzy and I had to sit down on a sofa. Then two men picked me up. I remember giggling a bit because I couldn't walk. My legs felt very heavy and they carried me upstairs.

I don't remember much after that. I remember bits but I'm not sure if it really happened or if it was a dream. I think I was lying on a bed looking up at a big chandelier and there was a man on top of me who was making love to me and another man who was kneeling next to me and telling me to suck him. I think I did suck him and then I was picked up and turned over so that I was face down on the bed and they lifted me up and pushed a pillow under me so that my bottom was in the air. One of the men got on top of me and pushed my legs apart and tried to push himself into my bum but I said that I didn't do anal then the other man grabbed my wrists and said something to me in Russian. I didn't understand what he said but he was angry and then he spat in my face. Then I think the door opened and Oliver and Cat were there, looking at what they were doing to me and I think that I begged them to help me but they didn't say anything and they didn't do anything and then they closed the door. The two Russians were laughing and that is the last thing I really remember until I woke up in my own bed. I was so sore and there were red marks everywhere like I'd been bitten. I lay down in a hot bath and tried to remember what had happened but I really can't remember anything else.

I phoned Nancy but her phone was turned off and I phoned Sandra but she didn't answer her phone. Then I phoned Dao and she answered and seemed really happy. She said that she had had a great time and that one of the men had tipped her £1,000. I think Dao is a bit crazy. I think she likes sex and drugs too much. I asked her if anyone had forced her to do anything she didn't want to and she just laughed and said that it had been fun. She asked me if I was okay and I lied and said that I was.

I think Oliver did a bad thing making us go to the party. I think he should have taken care of us. But I don't know what I can do. I have to work because I need money to pay Kung so I have to keep working for him. I can carry on doing this job but today I am sad, sad, sad, and I never want to go to the house in St John's Wood ever again.

Chapter 59

Monday June 15. Cat phoned me during the day and said that I should take my passport and Thai ID card to the flat in Sloane Square. I asked why and she said that it was because she and Oliver knew somebody who could get all our visas extended, which is good news.

I went to Sloane Square with Nancy and Sandra. Nancy had her passport and ID card and she was really excited because she had overstayed but Cat said that wouldn't be a problem and they could get that sorted out for her. Sandra didn't have her passport because she had posted it back to Thailand when her visa had expired. A lot of girls do that if they overstay. They send their passports back to Thailand in case they get caught by immigration in England. If they get caught they give a false name and they get sent home but nobody knows who they really are. Cat had told her to bring her ID card anyway.

England is a bit stupid about people who overstay. In Thailand the police put people who overstay in prison and fine them and make them pay for their own ticket out of the country. If they do not pay they stay in prison for ever. But in England they do not put people in prison for overstaying, they just give them a ticket to go. I think that is crazy, actually.

Candy had bought a copy of a local newspaper which talked about a gang being sent to prison for bringing prostitutes into London and we all read it and talked about it. There was a gang who were bringing in prostitutes and making them work in brothels in Paddington and Lancaster Gate which means that they were working near to my flat. The men in the gang were from Russia and their photographs were in the paper. They all looked quite normal, actually. Two of them weren't Russian, they were from China I think because they had Chinese names, Hui and Huang. The paper said that the police found drugs worth £100,000 in one of the flats of the gang. I think that drugs and working girls often go together. The paper said that the men were all arrested last year which was a long time before I started working for the agency. You know, it was quite funny because the police didn't arrest all the men and they were looking for one man and they caught him because he went to the court to watch the trial of his friends. Sometimes people can be so stupid, I think.

I feel very sorry for the girls that were forced to work in the brothels. That is the good thing about Oliver's agency. No one forces us to do this job. We all do it because we want to do it. We do it by choice. But the gang did not give the girls any choice. I am happy that they went to prison. The newspaper did not say what happened to the girls. I hope they were allowed to stay in England. It would not be fair if they were sent home, too.

When he took the money, Oliver gave everybody £300 back and said that was the fee for the party at St John's Wood. I took the money but I didn't say thank you or anything. I am fairly sure that Oliver put something in my drink at the party, and he knows that the Russian made love to me without a condom and he doesn't care. And I think he and Cat saw them forcing me to have anal, but I am not sure if that is a dream or not.

Dao was laughing a lot and saying that she wanted to go to another party like that because it was fun. I think she is a bit crazy. She has changed a lot and isn't like the girl I used to know. Before she was sweet and a bit shy but now I think she is just crazy. She lost a lot of money playing cards, too. More than £1,000. I lost £600 because I found it hard to concentrate.

Chapter 60

Thursday June 8. Sandra phoned me yesterday to say that she was really angry with Bee. Bee still hadn't paid her the money she owed her and now Bee has stopped answering the phone when she calls. Sandra said she wanted to go around to Bee's flat and talk to her and wanted me to go with her but I lied and said that I had a headache because I didn't want to get involved. Sandra kept asking me and said that Alice and Rachel were going with her and then I definitely didn't want to go because I know that Alice and Bee really hate each other and there will be trouble if they get together again.

A bit later Bee phoned me and asked me if she could come and talk to me and I said okay because actually I want to talk to her about working as an independent. I am still very unhappy with Oliver about what happened at the house in St John's Wood. Oliver is supposed to take care of me and he didn't at the St John's Wood house. He let the Russians do what they wanted and he didn't care. I don't see why I should give one third of everything I earn to Oliver if he doesn't take care of me.

Bee came around just before mid-day and she brought a whole watermelon for me which was really nice because she had remembered how much I like to eat it. I cut it in half and we ate half each, using spoons. That is the way I like to eat watermelon. It is much tastier than eating slices.

Bee had some big news for me. She said that she was stopping work as an escort. The rich American customer who gave her the Rolex watch wanted to take care of her and he had said that he would get a visa for her to go to America and get her an apartment in New York and that she would be his mistress which is like being a Mia Noi. Bee said the customer's name was Christopher and he had a good heart and a lot of money. Christopher had told her that one day he would leave his wife but that even if he didn't he would buy her the apartment and pay her a hundred thousand dollars a year and buy her anything she wanted. Bee laughed and said that Christopher really loved her. I asked her if she loved him and she said he had a good heart and he was rich and that was all that mattered. I asked her what would happen if she went to America and then Christopher changed his mind and Bee said that would never happen because she had used the magic perfume on him which meant that he would always want her, no matter what happened. She said that he was hers now until the day that he died, that whenever he thought about her he would want to have sex with her.

She said that if I wanted I could buy some of the perfume from her but actually I am not sure if I believe her. I think Robert and Simon both love me but it has nothing to do with magic. I think that maybe some men who use working girls find it too easy to lose their hearts. I think that is dangerous because some girls will take advantage of weak men. Actually that is what I think Bee is doing. I think she is taking advantage of Christopher.

I asked her if she was going to pay back Sandra the money for her contract and she said that maybe she would but she didn't have the cash just then. She said Christopher was giving her some money but not enough to pay all the money that she owed Sandra. Bee said that really it wasn't fair that she had to pay Sandra so much money. Sandra had only paid £6,000 for the contract but Bee was supposed to pay her back £18,000, which means a £12,000 profit for Sandra which is a lot of money. I didn't say anything because it isn't my business but I do think that a deal is a deal and Bee had a deal with Sandra so really she should pay her back.

Bee said that the reason that she wanted to talk to me was to ask me if I wanted to take over her website. Actually she wanted me to buy it. She said I could put my pictures on the website and that I could start working as an independent. She said I would make a lot more money than when I worked for the agency. I said I would think about it and actually I will because I think that maybe Oliver doesn't really care about the girls who work for him, I think he only cares about himself and about money. I used to think that Cat was my friend too but now I think that she is not really my friend. Bee said that if gave her £1,000 I could have her website and the mobile phone number. I think I will talk to Robert and ask him if he thinks it is a good idea. If I see Robert for four hours outcall he pays me £690 and I have to give £230 to

Oliver. If I was an independent then I would keep all the £690. I am sure that Robert would be my customer if I was an independent. So would Simon and Simon comes to see me at least twice a week and stays for three hours each time.

Bee asked me if I had read about the Russian gang who had been sent to prison for trafficking girls and I said yes, we had talked about it on Sunday and she asked me if I knew that they were friends of Oliver's and that was a surprise. I said I didn't know that and she said that she had been told it from a girl who worked for another agency. She said that before Covid a lot of working girls met at a Thai nightclub in Trafalgar Square called Thai Square and she used to go there every Friday night. She said that she met a girl who knew Oliver and she told Bee that actually Oliver has friends who work for the Russian Mafia and that I should be careful of him because he was a dangerous man. I am not sure if that is true. Oliver has always been very kind to me. Sometimes I think that Bee does not always tell the truth. Anyway, we ate the watermelon and we watched some Thai soap operas.

In the evening Richard came to see me again for an hour's incall but he only stayed forty minutes. Richard is the customer who tells his wife that he is out running but really he is in my flat having sex with me. He came in his tracksuit and running shoes and said that he had taken a taxi to my flat because it was quicker. I think it is more fun exercising with me than running around the streets. Actually, he is not having exercise, he is having sexercise!

My last customer was Vince and he came at just before midnight and booked me for two hours. I like Vince now. He is a customer but I think he is a real friend. He took cocaine while he was in my flat and asked me if I wanted some but I said no, I didn't like taking drugs and he said that was okay but that there was nothing wrong with cocaine so long as you didn't get addicted to it. I am not sure if that is true because if drugs were okay I don't think they would be illegal.

Chapter 61

Friday June 19. Yesterday I had two incall customers during the day. One was called Luke and he was quite nice. He said he worked in a pub but now he was out of a job and he said that he hadn't had sex for three months. I am not sure if that was true or not but he paid for two hours and had sex with me four times. I don't think he had taken Viagra either because his face wasn't red and he wasn't sniffing.

The second customer was called Jean and he was from France. He was quite young and said he was a lawyer and that he lived in Paris. He had booked me for two hours as well and asked me if I had any cocaine and I said I could get some so I called Vince and he brought some around to the flat and Jean paid him.

In the evening Simon booked me for four hours and he came around with a pizza. We watched two movies on Netflix and I opened a bottle of champagne. Then we went to the bedroom and I made love to him. I wish that I had more feeling with Simon but he is so small that there is no feeling at all and I am always worried that the condom will come off. That is the funny thing about condoms. In the shops they only sell one size but men are actually all different sizes. Do you know, I have seen hundreds of men naked and there is a lot of difference between the biggest and the smallest but there is only one size of condom. I suppose that if they did make them in different sizes the men who needed the small size would be too shy to buy them.

Simon left at one o'clock in the morning and I thought I would be finished for the night but at two o'clock Oliver phoned and said that I had an incall booking for ninety minutes at half past two. I was so tired that I just wanted to sleep and then I remembered that Jean had left behind a little bit of cocaine. He had used most of it but there was some left and he had forgotten to take it with him. I had actually thrown it away but I got it out of the bin and sniffed it. It was the first time I had ever sniffed cocaine and the feeling was totally different from licking it. It is difficult to explain how it felt but it stopped me from feeling sleepy. I felt like I had a lot of energy and at one point the customer said I was making love to him so hard that I was hurting him. I thought that was funny and I laughed a lot and he said that I was crazy.

His name was Eddie and he said that he had been arguing with his wife because she had been unfaithful so he had slept with me to make her feel bad. His wife had left home and was living with another man, he said, so really I am not sure that he is sleeping with a working girl. I felt a bit sorry for him and I gave him my phone number and said that I hoped he would come to see me again. After Eddie had gone I tried to sleep but I couldn't because my heart was beating so fast so I lay on the sofa and watched Netflix movies all night.

Chapter 62

Saturday June 20. I put more money into DVD cases and posted them to my mum in Thailand. This time I sent £3,000 in fifty pound notes.

Oliver phoned me at mid-day to say that I had a booking for domination with Candy again. It was for two hours starting at one o'clock so I went straight around to her apartment to get ready. Candy was wearing a red plastic dress with holes cut out for her breasts and thigh-length black plastic boots and she had painted her nails a bright red and she had on bright red nail varnish. Actually she looked very sexy. She helped me get changed into a very strange dress that was just strips of leather held together by studs that showed off most of my body. She gave me a pair of thigh-length boots and I put them on then she put lipstick on me. Lots of lipstick. Then we stood and looked at each other in the mirror and said that we both looked very sexy. The customer was called Walter and he worked for a bank. I thought about asking him about how I could open a bank account in England but after I had seen what Candy did to him I didn't want to ask him for his advice. He wanted Candy to use a strap on him while I held him down. He kept begging her to stop but he didn't use the safe word which meant that really he didn't want her to stop. The strap on was so big that it must have really hurt. He kept calling her Mistress which was quite funny. Mistress can be the same as Mia Noi, a girl that a married man takes care of, but in domination Mistress means something else. Mistress means that she has power over the man.

Candy told me that sometimes men liked a woman to have power over them, especially men who are in important jobs. They spend all day telling people what to do and to relax they want someone to tell them what to do. But I do not understand why he wants a dildo up his bum. I think that maybe he is gay and that really he wants a man to do it to his bum.

Candy spent thirty minutes doing that to him, then she tied him to the bed and put a blindfold on him and then we both hit him with leather whips. Candy made him beg us to hit him and every time we did he had to say 'thank you, Mistress.'

While we were doing it Candy talked to me in Thai, telling me about the last time she went shopping with Alice and Rachel and the fun that they had. I think the customer would be annoyed if he knew what we were talking about because we were supposed to be working but Candy said that he didn't understand Thai.

Candy said that Walter liked to make himself come but he wanted to do that while she dominated me. She had done it before with Nancy and was I okay and I said sure, so long as it didn't hurt too much. She took the blindfold off him and untied him, then he helped tie me up and Candy hit me with a leather whip as Walter sat in a chair and made himself come. Then she made him kneel down in front of us and kiss our feet and thank us. He must have really enjoyed it because he gave us both a £100 tip.

After Walter had gone I used Candy's bathroom to shower. I went to pee and it itched a little bit when I peed and I had a white discharge which I think is not a good thing. I asked Candy what she thought and she said that it was nothing to worry about and that maybe I had been eating too much spicy food. Maybe she was right. It only itched a bit and it's not as if it hurt or anything. Maybe it will go away on its own.

I went home and I had two customers for incall, one at six o'clock and one at eight o'clock. The first one was called Ryan and the second was called Danny and it was funny because they were both from Ireland and they both looked the same with black hair and blue eyes. Now when I think back I can't even remember which is which. I asked them both for their phone numbers and told them that I really liked them and wanted them to come back and see me again.

Bee phoned me at ten o'clock and asked me if I wanted to meet some girls who work for another agency, the ones she used to meet in Thai Square before Covid. I said yes. I sent Oliver a text saying that I had a bad stomach and that I couldn't work any more that night and then I got changed and ordered an Uber taxi.

When I got to Bee's flat she was with two pretty girls. Their names were Poy and Fun and Bee said they worked for A1 which is the biggest Asian agency in London. They were quite pretty but had very dark skin. I think they were from Isarn. Bee asked them about the girl who had been attacked and they said that she was still in hospital. Luckily in England when you are in hospital you don't have to pay because in Thailand you have to pay a lot of money when you are very sick. Poy said that she had heard that two other girls had been attacked and the police had a picture of what they thought he looked like but they still hadn't caught him. I told her about the policeman who had come to see me and Fun said that he had come to see her, too. The police really care about the working girls in London. The police in London are really nice, I think. In Thailand you have to be careful of the police. If you have an enemy and he has friends who are policemen then you have a big problem. Bee told Poy and Fun that she was giving up work and that her big American customer was going to take care of her. They squealed and hugged her and told her how lucky she was. Poy said that was the dream of a lot of working girls, to find a man who can take care of them. But that is not my dream. I want to work and make money so that I can help my family myself.

Then another girl arrived. Her name was Moon and she worked for A1, too. Bee introduced me and said that Moon used to work for Oliver but she had stopped after a customer had forced her to have sex without a condom. Moon had complained to Oliver but Oliver said there was nothing he could do about it but Moon found out that the customer was a friend of Oliver's and that he was from Russia. The customer was one of the men who had just been sent to prison, said Moon. Oliver was a bad man, she said, and he worked for the Russian mafia. She said it would be better for me if I did not work for Oliver because he did not care about his girls, he only cared about money. I did not know what to say because Oliver has always been good to me but it is true that he didn't help me when I complained about what had happened in the house in St John's Wood.

They talked about Thai Square and how sad they were because it had to close.The girls said that the bar was a good place to meet Asian guys and even farangs and that the men usually didn't know that they were working girls. I said that I didn't want to meet farangs or Asian men because I didn't want to FFF, I just wanted to work. The girls wanted to know what FFF meant and I told them it meant Fuck For Free and they all laughed at that. Fon said that she never did FFF. Even if she met a guy who didn't know that she was a working girl she could still get him to spend a lot of money on her. She showed us the Cartier watch she was wearing and said that a guy she had met in Thai Square had bought it for her. It was a nice watch.

We had a really good time, eating and laughing and sharing stories about our customers. It almost made me forget about the problems I was having with Oliver and Kung.

Chapter 63

Sunday June 21. Yesterday I saw a VIP customer. That is what Oliver called him but I didn't recognise him. It wasn't like when Nancy and I saw the famous actor. But he was a VIP that is for sure because he had bodyguards, a lot of bodyguards.

Oliver said that I had a VIP customer at a house in Belgravia and that I should wear something smart. Oliver said the customer would pay me in dollars and that was okay. He should give me $800.

I took an Uber taxi to the house. It was huge, a mansion. I rang the doorbell and after a few minutes a very good looking man in a black suit opened it. My heart actually turned over he was so good looking and I thought he was the customer and I was very happy but he wasn't the customer, he was a bodyguard. He had a thing in his ear and once he put his hand to his mouth and spoke into his sleeve which looked quite funny. As he spoke to me I saw two other men watching us. They wore good suits too and had things in their ears. I went up in the lift with the good-looking bodyguard. Yes, the house was so big there was a real lift in it. He didn't say anything to me in the lift and even though I smiled sweetly at him and asked him his name he just looked at me. I think he was smiling a bit, though. I wondered what he would do if I knelt down and gave him a blow job, but that was just me thinking crazy like I do sometimes.

The bodyguard took me down a corridor where there was a man and a woman who were both smartly dressed and with the same things in their ears. The woman was holding a black walkie-talkie. Neither of them smiled at me but the woman opened the door and nodded for me to go inside.

The room was huge. The biggest I have ever seen outside of a hotel. And the furniture was lovely, the sort of things you see in the furniture department in Harrods. There was no bed but there were three doors so I guess they led to where the bedrooms where. The VIP was quite old, maybe sixty or more, with grey hair combed back. Actually he looked a bit like Bill Clinton but honestly it was not Bill Clinton. I did not recognise him at all, actually, but he must have been very important because he had so many bodyguards. He was wearing a bathrobe that was quite short so I could see his knobbly knees. He didn't say anything, he just gave me an envelope and I looked inside and there were ten $100 notes. I said that he only had to pay me $800 and he said that there was a $200 tip. That was a surprise because usually the customer gives me a tip afterwards but giving me the tip first was okay.

The VIP took off his robe. His body wasn't very nice. It was actually older looking than his face and there were red patches on his thighs that didn't look healthy. His dick was very big. Very, very, big. But it wasn't hard. He told me to get undressed and I did and then he told me to give him a blow job and I did. He got hard very quickly which was a surprise because usually old men take a long time to get hard. He was quite rough and held my head and pushed himself deep into me which I don't like but I let him do it. Then he told me to get on the bed and he made love to me doggy-style which hurt a lot. I told him he was hurting me but he didn't care, in fact he did it harder. He was so deep inside me that I was crying a bit. I remembered what Nancy had said when she had seen the man with the big dick in the sexy movie we saw in the house in St John's Wood about the dick banging her chin but actually a big dick is not that funny if the guy is not gentle.

Then he told me to lie on my back and he put a pillow under my bum to raise me up a bit and he made love to me hard again. The pillow meant that he went deeper inside me and it hurt a lot but he didn't care. Actually his face looked quite angry as he was having sex and he kept swearing and saying something that sounded like 'gook' which I don't understand but which I don't think is a good word. He grunted when he came and then he rolled off and was breathing so heavily that I thought he was having a heart attack.

After he had come I went to the bathroom to pee and it itched again, more than before and I still had the white discharge. I didn't eat anything spicy the night before so I don't think it was anything to do with what I had to eat. I am not sure what to do because I am scared that if I go to a doctor they will want to know what I do for a living and I don't want to tell them that I am a working girl. I might go to a chemists and ask if they have some medicine but I don't want to go to the pharmacy near my flat because the Indian guy is there who keeps saying 'Sawasdee krup' and I don't want to talk to him.

When I came out of the bathroom the VIP had put his robe back on and he was talking on the phone. He lowered his phone when I came out as if he didn't want me to overhear. The good-looking bodyguard took me down in the lift to the front door where there was a taxi waiting for me. He actually opened the door of a taxi for me, which was very polite. I sort of hoped that he would ask me for my phone number, but he didn't.

When I was in the taxi back to my flat I phoned Oliver to tell him that everything was okay and he told me that I had a two-hour incall booking. It was Jean, the French lawyer who had seen me on Thursday. I was actually pleased that Jean had booked me again because he was nice and his accent was quite sexy. You know, he brought flowers to give me, they were lilies that smelled really sweet. He gave me the flowers and kissed me on the cheek like we were on a date. But he gave me my money right away and I put it on the coffee table then opened a bottle of wine for him. We kissed on the sofa and I gave him oral, soft and slow and then he said he wanted to make love to me on the sofa so we did, though first I had to get a condom from the bedroom.

Then he asked me if I could get him some more cocaine and I called Vince. Vince said it would take him an hour to get to Bayswater and I told that to Jean and he said okay, no problem, and that he would book me for another two hours. I was so pleased because that meant I had worked for two hours outcall and four hours incall in one day which meant good money and only two customers. I phoned Oliver and told him that Jean wanted two hours more and Oliver said okay and said that Jean could have a discount for the second two hours. Oliver said he was a good customer and had been with most of the girls at the agency which made me a bit unhappy because I thought maybe I was special.

I had a bath with him and then I gave him oral in the bedroom until Vince came. Jean gave me £300 and I gave £200 to Vince and gave the cocaine to Jean. Jean put the cocaine on the coffee table and made it into lines and he sniffed two and then asked me if I wanted some. I was going to say no but then I realised I was a bit tired after having sex with the VIP so I said yes, I would have some. I sniffed one line up each nostril and almost immediately I was not tired. In fact I felt full of energy. We made love on the sofa and it was only when he was inside me that I remembered that he had not put a condom on. I told him to stop but he said he couldn't and then I thought that it was probably okay because he was a good customer and anyway he was already inside me so I carried on. Actually, there is more feeling when there is no condom so I do understand why some men don't want to use them. I asked him not to come inside me and he said okay and just before he came he pulled himself out and came over my stomach. Jean is a good man and I hope he will be a regular customer. I didn't ask him for his phone number last time but this time I did and before I went to sleep I sent him a text message saying that I had enjoyed my time with him and that I missed him. Then I sent the same message to another ten customers.

Chapter 64

Monday June 22. Wanda phoned me yesterday morning and asked if I would go to her apartment because Nancy and Sandra were going and they were going to talk to Julie. I said I would even though I really didn't want to. Actually I wanted to ask the girls about the itch and the discharge I had so I bought a watermelon and some oranges and I took that around to Wanda's flat.

They already had the letters around the glass but we ate the fruit first and talked about our customers. I told them about Vince and how he could get cocaine for customers if they wanted but Wanda and Sandra said they already had customers who could get cocaine for them. Sandra said she quite liked taking cocaine but she never paid for it herself, she would only use it if her customer bought some. Wanda told me about a film producer who had been seeing her for months. His name was Paul and he liked to make breakfast for her, muesli and bananas. It sounded to me like he was a bit like Robert and liked to take care of girls. Wanda said he couldn't make love, he could only come when she played with him and that sounded a bit like Robert too, except Robert plays with himself. Men can be strange sometimes. Sandra told us about an American singer who comes to see her who has the biggest dick she has ever seen, bigger than a man's arm, she said, but Sandra often exaggerates. Nancy told us about two teenagers who come to see her. They are brothers and actually only one of them phones to book her but they both come to see her. Nancy was laughing and said that actually she would FFF because they were such good fun.

I told the girls about my problem and Sandra said that when she had a problem she went to see a Chinese doctor in Chinatown who gave her some herbs that stopped her itching. I am not sure if I trust Chinese doctors, though. I asked them what they thought was wrong and they said I probably had an infection and that I must have got it from a customer. Nancy said she never got sick but I don't believe that because she makes love without a condom. I know that it must have happened at the house at St John's Wood so it is Oliver's fault that I am sick. Wanda said it could be lots of things like a fungal infection which meant I had to take some tablets or it might be an STD. She didn't know what STD meant but it was something you catch from a customer. STD can be fixed with antibiotics. In Thailand you can buy antibiotics in any pharmacy but in England you have to get them from a doctor, she said. I said I didn't know any doctors in London and she said she had a card for a clinic in Harley Street and she gave me a business card. I asked if they would want to know about my job but Wanda said that they didn't care, all they care about is money. But she wasn't sure if they would be open because of Covid. A lot of doctors were refusing to see sick people because they were so scared of catching the virus.

When we had finished the fruit we sat around the coffee table and put our hands on the glass. It started to move in small circles and Wanda asked if there was anyone there and the glass moved to 'YES'. Then she asked who was there and it spelled out J-U-L-I-A which was strange because last time it was Julie. Wanda asked her to spell it again and the glass moved to spell J-U-L-I-E so we knew it was her. Then the glass slowly spelled out T-H-A-N-K Y-O-U F-O-R T-H-E P-R-E-S-E-N-T-S.

Nancy asked if Julie wanted anything else and the glass spelled out T-E-D-D-Y B-A-R-E. Actually I thought that was strange because a Teddy Bear is B-E-A-R and not B-A-R-E. Maybe Julie can't spell but I think a young farang girl would know how to spell bear. But I know that Nancy isn't very good at spelling and neither is Sandra so one of them could be pushing the glass.

Wanda then said that last time Julie had said there was danger and the glass moved to 'YES.' Wanda asked who was in danger and the glass spelled out E-V-E-R-Y-O-N-E. That was a bit scary actually. I was looking very carefully at everybody's fingers but I didn't see anyone pushing. When we started we were laughing and joking but now we weren't laughing.

Wanda asked where the danger was coming from and the glass spelled out O-L-I-V-E-R. We all stared at the glass on the letter R. Why would there be danger from Oliver? That didn't make any sense.

Wanda asked why but the glass didn't move. She asked why again and then the glass spelled out C-O-L-D. Then it spelled out D-A-R-K. Then it stopped. Then it spelled out D-A-N-G-E-R.

Then the phone rang and it was Oliver. Can you believe it? It was exactly the same as happened last time. Oliver said that Wanda had a booking so we all had to go.

I went to Sloane Square on my own this time. Alice, Rachel, Candy and Vicky were already there, cooking with Cat in the kitchen. Oliver was drinking beer and watching the television.

Alice asked when we would be getting our passports and ID cards back but Oliver said he didn't know, he was still talking to his contact about getting us visas. Actually when he said that he looked uncomfortable and I think maybe he was lying. But Cat smiled and told us not to worry, that everything was okay. Then we played cards and we all lost money, except for Oliver who was lucky, as usual.

Chapter 65

Tuesday June 23. Yesterday I was busy, busy, busy. I had six customers during the day. Once I had one customer going down in the lift as another customer was coming up and I hardly had any time to shower. One of the six was Vince, which was good because time with Vince is always fun. He looks a bit rough but he has a very good heart and I think he really cares about me. He says he is earning very good money selling drugs and unless he does something stupid he says that the police will never catch him. I though all drugs were controlled by the mafia but Vince says he works for himself. He buys his drugs from an Irish man who he has known for years and he only sells to people that he knows. It's not as if he walks around the streets trying to sell drugs. It isn't like that. People phone him up and he delivers, like a pizza service. Most people don't even know his name, they just call him The Candyman. In a way our jobs are very similar. The police don't really care about what we do unless we make a nuisance of ourselves.

Vince was very gentle with me when he made love to me, like he always is. He's quite tender and he kisses my neck and whispers my name which is nice. I told him my name the second time he came to see me. Actually I tell all my customers my name because it is only my nickname. All Thai people have a real name which is on their passports and ID cards and all documents, but they also have a nickname that is the name that most people use. Actually Thai people can have several nicknames. Like my mother and father call me Jar which means sweet but my schoolfriends call me Porn and my grandmother, my Yai, has another name for me. It can be confusing sometimes!

Actually yesterday I wanted to go to see the doctor about my itch and my discharge but I was just too busy. I phoned Wanda to see if she would go with me but she said that she was too busy, too. I think everyone is busy at the moment. Maybe the cold weather makes people horny. In fact the weather does make a difference to how busy we are. If it is raining we do not get many customers and if it is very hot like it was for one week in the summer then we don't get many customers. The best day is actually a cold, dry day and yesterday was a cold, dry day.

My first customer came at mid-day. His name was John, but I don't think that was his real name. A lot of customers say they are called John. Or Dave. They are the two most popular names of my customers. John didn't talk to me and didn't look me in the eye no matter how much I smiled. When we were on the bed he had his eyes closed most of the time, so maybe he was thinking about someone else.

My second customer was called Steve and he was a bit fat and didn't smell very good so I spent a long time in the bath with him to make sure that he was clean. Actually I made love to him in the bath, and I made sure that he came so that all I had to do in the bedroom was to give him a massage.

Then Sandra phoned me to say she was very angry with Bee because she hadn't paid her the money for the contract. I think she will be much more angry if she knows that Bee is going to live in New York, but I didn't say anything.

I phoned Bee but she didn't answer my call and then Oliver phoned me to say that I had another booking. He was a new customer and after he had gone I phoned Bee and told her that Sandra wanted to talk to her. Bee laughed and said that she didn't want to talk to her. Really I don't think Bee is being fair because she does owe money to Sandra. But Sandra owes me money and she never mentions it so maybe it is fair. The English have a saying. What goes around comes around. So what Sandra is doing to me, Bee is doing to her.

I told Bee about my itch and my discharge and she said that I might have gonorrhoea which needs treating very quickly but is easy to cure. She said that she knew a good doctor that was a woman who has a surgery near her apartment and she was still seeing patients. She said she would go with me which was really nice of her. I said I would go around to her place in the morning.

The last customer of the day was Robert so I didn't eat anything during the afternoon so that I would be hungry when he gave me his peanut butter sandwiches. He is always happier when I eat all the sandwich and drink my milk shake. I do wish he would let me do something for him to show how grateful I am for his help but he keeps telling me that all he wants to do is to kiss my feet. He is a strange man but he has a very good heart.

Chapter 66

Wednesday June 24. I woke up early yesterday so I did two on-line lessons with my school and then I had some watermelon to eat and then I phoned Bee to see if she wanted to go to see the doctor with me but her phone was switched off. I showered and called her again and her phone was still switched off and I thought that maybe her battery had died because that sometimes happens to me so I put on my coat and walked around to her apartment. I was so shocked when I got to the road where her apartment was because there were two police cars there and an ambulance and there were strips of tape around the lampposts to keep people away. There were lots of uniformed policemen around and I knew straight away that something was wrong. There were some people standing near the police cars watching but I didn't want to stand too close so I stood outside a shop and pretended to be looking in the window. After a bit another car arrived and parked next to the police cars. Two men got out and one of them was Neil, the policeman that had come to see me, and I knew then for sure that something had happened to Bee. Neil and the other man went inside the building. They were both wearing facemasks. I had a really bad feeling in my stomach like I was going to be sick. The ambulance was just waiting and there was no siren or anything so it wasn't as if she was ill and they were rushing her to the hospital. Then a white van arrived and three people got out in white paper suits and hoods and they were carrying big black cases and they went inside.

I wanted to phone somebody and talk about it but I couldn't because I didn't want Oliver and Cat and Sandra to know that I was going to see Bee. I stayed in front of the shop shivering because it was cold but I didn't want to go home. After about an hour two men came out with a stretcher and there was something on the stretcher and I was sure that it was Bee's body. They put it in the ambulance and then they drove off but they weren't in a hurry. I went home then and I cried and I cried and I cried.

I don't know what happened but all I can think is that the robber who was stealing from working girls killed her and that was why Neil was there. It was so unfair because she had stopped work and she was going to go to New York. I really liked Bee, she was actually a very nice girl and she had a good heart.

I watched the six o'clock news on television but there was nothing about a girl being killed. I couldn't eat or anything, I was so worried. I wanted to talk to somebody but I didn't know who I could talk to. I know that Robert would want to help but he is a good man and I don't want to worry him about my problem. I thought about phoning Neil the policeman but he might not know that Bee had worked for Oliver's agency and if he knew then he might want to talk to Oliver and Oliver might be angry at me. I was thinking so much that I got sick and I threw up in the bathroom. Then I started crying because I was sad, sad, sad. And I was a bit scared too.

There was only one person I could think of ringing and that was Vince. I phoned him and I started crying and he said that he would come around to see me and he did, he was there after twenty minutes and he was very worried about me. He sat on the sofa and held me while I cried. I told him what had happened and he said that he was sorry. He was so gentle and kind. He is a real friend. I asked him why there hadn't been a story on the television. He said television didn't usually report murders unless it was someone important or unless children were hurt. There were more than two hundred murders every year in London, he said. And he said that sometimes the police kept the details quiet because they didn't want anyone to know about their investigation. He asked me if I was sure that Bee had been murdered and I told him everything that I had seen and I showed him what happened when I phoned her number. The phone was still switched off. I said that I was sure but he said that he would go around in the morning and ask some questions and see what he could find out.

You know, Vince was so kind. He didn't try to kiss me or do anything, he just held me and talked to me. He was just what I needed, a real friend who cares about me. He stayed with me all night and we lay on the bed together and he held me and told me that everything would be okay even though I know it won't be okay because nothing will bring Bee back.

Chapter 67

Thursday June 25. I hardly slept last night. Vince did and he snored a bit but that was okay because even if I had my eyes closed I didn't feel as if I was alone. He went out in the morning and came back with croissants for breakfast but really I wasn't hungry. I phoned Bee's number but her phone was still off. At about eleven o'clock Vince said that I should show him where Bee's flat is so I went with him. All the police tape had gone and it was as if it had never happened. I showed Vince where the flat was and where to press the bell and he said that I should go home because it wouldn't be good for another Thai girl to be seen nearby so I did what he said.

About half an hour later he came to my flat. This time he had brought two coffees and a whole watermelon with him. It was so nice of him to remember that I liked watermelon and actually I did manage to eat some even though my stomach did not feel good at all. Vince said that he had rung Bee's bell but that no one had answered. Then he rang a neighbour's bell and a neighbour said that yes, a girl had been killed and that she was Asian. Vince said the neighbour didn't know how the girl was killed because the police weren't saying. Vince said there was no CCTV at the entrance to the flat so the police wouldn't know who had been to the building. I am surprised that Bee didn't live in a building with CCTV because all working girls need CCTV to be safe.

I am worried about Bee's family because I am not sure if the police would know who she is or where she is from. When a girl comes to England on a contract that somebody has paid, she usually has to give her passport to her sponsor for security. That means that Sandra will have Bee's passport and maybe her ID card too. If Bee rented her room in her own name then the police would know who she is but a lot of working girls don't use their real names. I don't know what to do because if I contact Neil to tell him what I know then maybe I will get Sandra and Oliver angry at me and I do not want that.

At noon Oliver phoned me to say that I had a booking for one o'clock. I didn't want to work but I had no reason to say no so I said yes. He asked me if I was feeling okay and I said I was fine, that my stomach wasn't hurting any more. He didn't sound as if he was happy with me,

Before the customer came, Vince went out and got two free newspapers. We read them both but there was nothing about a girl being killed in Paddington. There was a story about an Arab boy who had been shot and the police were asking for anyone who had seen anything to call them. I don't understand why there wasn't a story about Bee in the paper. In Thailand if there is a murder the Thai newspapers have photographs on the front page. You can see the blood and everything. Actually it is quite gory. Vince said that the police might know who the killer is so they keep the story out of the papers so that they won't scare him off. I didn't understand that but I think that Vince knows more about the police than I do.

He went just before my first customer came. During the day I had six customers, all of them incall and all of them for one hour. I had sex with six men and I earned £600 for me and £300 for Oliver. I was tired and sore when I had finished, which was at three o'clock in the morning. I was too tired to send good night texts to my customers but I did send one to Vince to thank him for being such a good friend. I did sleep but I kept having bad dreams, mostly about somebody killing Bee with a knife.

Chapter 68

Friday June 26. I was very busy yesterday. So was Vince. He phoned twice during the day to see if I was okay which was nice of him.

My first customer came at eleven o'clock which is early because usually customers come after mid-day. I was actually quite tired because I didn't sleep much the night before. I had two more customers in the afternoon, both incall. I was running out of condoms so I went to buy some. I looked through the window of the pharmacy and I didn't see the Indian guy so I went inside but you know what, just as I was at the cash register he came up behind me and said 'Sawasdee krup' and made me jump. Then he looked at the twelve dozen condoms in my basket and the KY Jelly and he smiled like he knew what I was doing. I really hate him so I just paid for what I had bought and didn't say anything to him.

At six o'clock Oliver phoned and told me that I had an incall booking from a new customer and that Simon had booked me for three hours incall at ten o'clock. I barely had time to think all day, which was a good thing really because every time I think about Bee I feel sad, sad, sad.

I FaceTimed my mother I spoke to Ice and he kept saying that he missed me and wanted me to go back to Thailand and then I started to cry so I had to cut the phone call short because I didn't want him to be upset.

Simon left at one o'clock in the morning. He kept asking me to be his girlfriend and to stop work, which is a bit boring actually.

At two o'clock in the morning Wanda phoned me, very excited. She said that Julie had come to talk to them again and that this time she had said that she had been murdered. Can you believe that? Julie said that it was her own mother who had killed her by smothering her with a pillow. I am not sure if they are really talking to a ghost, I think it is more likely to be someone pushing the glass, probably Sandra, but I didn't tell Wanda.

Chapter 69

Saturday June 27. When I woke up yesterday morning I was itching a lot and there was a white discharge again so I phoned Wanda and asked if she would go with me to see her doctor and she said that she wasn't busy so she would. I went around to her apartment. The glass was still on the coffee table and she said that Julie had spent ages talking to them. Everyone was very sad. Nancy had bought a teddy bear for her and Julie said thank you for that but then Sandra wanted to know how Julie had died and that was when the whole story came out. I asked Wanda if Julie had said anything more about danger and she said no because they were all interested in how Julie had died. Julie had said that she didn't know why her mother had killed her with the pillow but said that her father had left home when she was a baby. Actually I still think that it is all a joke, that someone is pushing the glass but I didn't say that to Wanda because I know she believes in it. But I did buy her the doll called Julie because if she is real I do not want her to be sad.

Wanda had phoned to make an appointment at the clinic she uses and they weren't busy and said we could go at eleven o'clock. We got a taxi to Harley Street and the doctor was a handsome man from New Zealand who was really sweet and didn't ask me about my job. He tested me for everything including Aids and gave me a full examination and that was funny because I was lying on my back with my legs wide open and usually when I am like that the man is paying me but this time I was paying him. I kept laughing because it was funny and he thought he was tickling me and kept saying sorry. What also was funny was that he asked me some questions which he said he had to ask me before he could give me the Aids test and one of the questions was how many men I had had sex with in the last six months. I think if I told him the truth that he would be very shocked so I just lied and said three.

He said I didn't have gonorrhoea which was good news, or syphilis, but he said I did have Chlamydia which I probably caught from a man with NSU which is an STD. STD stands for sexually transmitted disease but I don't know what NSU stands for but the doctor says it was not serious and I just need to take antibiotics for ten days and just to be on the safe side he would give me an injection too. He said I should tell my sexual contacts that I have Chlamydia and that if they are worried they should go to the doctor to be checked but I don't think I can tell all my customers that I have an STD because then they will think that I am not professional.

When we were going home Wanda asked me what I thought about Oliver taking our passports and our ID cards and I said I thought it was okay if it meant we got new visas but she said she was a bit worried because if the police caught her then she would be in trouble because she didn't have her passport. I said I didn't think Oliver would keep them for long.

Actually I wanted to talk to Wanda about Bee but I thought that if I did she might tell Cat and I would get into trouble.

I had two outcall jobs and three incall jobs. Simon phoned to tell me that he had tried to book me for three hours but that he had been told that I was busy all evening and I said that yes that was true. Simon was sad but there was nothing I could do. The first customer to book me gets me, I cannot cancel a booking just because a regular customer wants to see me.

At midnight I phoned Nancy to see if she was busy and she said that she was. She said she had spoken to Sandra and that Sandra was very busy too. Nancy said that Candy was having her period and that Vicky had cold sores all over her lips so neither of them could work and Oliver was giving us their customers. I asked Nancy if her period had come yet and she said that it hadn't. I asked her if she was worried that she might be pregnant but she said she didn't care and anyway her customers wouldn't be able to tell. You know, if she is pregnant I don't think she will know who the father is, which I think is quite bad really.

By the time I had finished work I was really tired and I had earned more than £850. Do you know how much money I have hidden under the carpet now? Actually I shouldn't tell anyone because it is a lot. I will send some more to my mother and I will ask Vince if he can send some to my bank. It is not a good idea to have too much money in my flat.

Chapter 70

Sunday June 28. Yesterday I went to eat Thai food and watch Thai soap operas at Candy's flat with Wanda, Sandra, Dao and Nancy.

After we had eaten, Wanda told Candy about talking to Julie using the glass and the letters and Candy and Dao said that she wanted to try it. I didn't really want to but Sandra and Nancy said it was fun and so we did it. Sandra cut up pieces of paper and Nancy wrote down the letters and 'YES' and 'NO' and 'DON'T KNOW'. The we put the pieces of paper in a big circle on Candy's table and the 'YES' and 'NO' and 'DON'T KNOW' in the middle. Then we sat around the table and put our fingers on the glass. Candy asked what happened next and Wanda said that we just waited for a spirit.

Actually nothing happened for about five minutes and I was getting bored and I wanted to watch television. But just as I was going to take my finger off the glass it started to move. At first it just moved from side to side a bit but then it started to move in small circles. Sandra asked if there was anybody there and the glass moved really quickly over to 'YES'. Candy's eyes were so wide that I almost laughed and Dao looked really surprised.

Nancy asked if there was a message for us and the glass moved to the middle of the circle and then shot over to 'YES' again. I could feel the glass pulling but I wasn't sure if anyone was pushing it or not. I am sure that Candy wasn't pushing because she was too surprised and I know that I wasn't.

Dao was laughing and asking if it always happened and Nancy said yes, it did. If there were spirits around then they always wanted to talk to living people.

Candy asked what the message was and the glass spelled out a word. It spelled D-A-N-G-E-R which is what Julie said in Wanda's flat.

Sandra asked who was in danger and the glass spelled out E-V-E-R-Y-B-O-D-Y. That is the message we got last time.

Nancy asked if Julie was happy with the teddy bear she had bought but the glass didn't move. She asked again but the glass stayed where it was. Then Nancy asked if Julie was there and the glass moved really quickly over to 'NO' and that is when I got a bit scared.

Sandra asked who was there and the glass moved really slowly over to the letter B and I knew right away what it was going to spell. And sure enough, really slowly, it spelled out B-E-E. Everyone was shocked then. Except for Dao. She wanted to know who Bee was and I told her that she was a girl who used to work for Oliver.

Then Candy said that the game was only to speak to dead people so it couldn't be Bee because Bee wasn't dead. I didn't want to tell them that actually Bee was dead so I just stayed quiet. Nancy said that maybe Bee had died and she had something to tell us. So she asked if it was Bee who used to work for Oliver and the glass shot across the table to 'YES'. Nancy asked if Bee was dead and the glass went slowly to the middle of the table and then shot back to 'YES' again.

Candy asked what had happened to Bee and the glass didn't move. Candy asked again and the glass started to move. It spelled out M-U-R-D and then it was just moving to the letter E when Sandra stood up. She shouted at me that I was pushing the glass which wasn't true and then she picked up the glass and threw it against the wall and then pushed all the letters off the table. I was shocked because honestly I wasn't pushing the glass. Sandra was really angry and I thought she was going to hit me but she left the flat and Nancy went after her. I was really upset and I started crying and Candy and Wanda and Dao all hugged me and said that it wasn't my fault which was true but I don't understand why Sandra was so angry.

Chapter 71

Monday June 29. Yesterday when we went to the Sloane Square flat there was another man there. It was the first time that I had ever seen another man at the flat. Oliver said that his name was Sacha and that he was a friend and I remember seeing him at the party at the house in St John's Wood. Sacha is about thirty I think and he has short spiky hair and bad skin like he had lots of spots when he was a kid. He didn't smile and he had very hard eyes like they were made of brown ice. He sat on the sofa and drank beer from the bottle and all the time he was watching, watching, watching.

When we gave our money to Oliver I saw Sacha watching carefully and I saw Cat looking at him all the time like she was worried what he might say. After we had all given Oliver our money, Cat brought out some Thai food that she had cooked – Pad Thai and Tom Yam Gung which is spicy prawn soup, and Som Tam, green papaya salad, which is very very spicy and which all Thai people love to eat. Cat asked Sacha if he wanted to eat some and he just shook his head like he was angry.

Sacha stayed on the sofa while we sat at the table and ate the food, which was delicious. Then we played cards. Oliver showed Sacha how to play and then he started to relax a bit and even laughed when he won. Actually he was quite lucky and won a lot of money, more than £500. Oliver won, too. I lost about £700 and Sandra lost even more. While we played Alice asked Sacha where he was from and he said Russia.

Dao was drinking a lot and being a bit silly. She kept touching Sacha and blowing him kisses and actually he seemed to like it.

Rachel asked Cat when we could be getting our passports back and something very strange happened. Right away Cat looked at Sacha, as if Sacha was the boss now. It was only for a second or two but I realised that something had changed and that Cat and Oliver were no longer in charge and actually I was a bit scared, more scared then when Bee's ghost had come to talk to us. I think something bad is going to happen. Something really bad.

Then Cat smiled and said soon. We would get our passports back soon and we would all have one year visas that would allow us to work. Everyone clapped and cheered except me. I just smiled even though I didn't feel like smiling.

Chapter 72

Wednesday July 1. I phoned Vince on Monday and asked him if he would come to my flat because I wanted to talk to him about my money. I was busy during the evening and so was he so he didn't come until two o'clock in the morning and we were both very tired. I said that I wanted to send £10,000 back to my bank account in Udon Thani and he said he would help me but that it wasn't a good idea to send so much at the same time. He said the banks got suspicious if someone sent £10,000 and they would tell the tax people or the police. It was better to send less than £5,000. It wasn't a problem but he would send two lots of money just to be on the safe side and that was okay. You know, Vince was the first man I have asked to my room who was not a customer. But now I don't really think that Vince is a customer, he is a friend. I got ten envelopes from under the carpet behind the sofa and gave them to him.

Vince took out some cocaine and asked me if I wanted some and I said okay because I was so tired and thought I might fall asleep. He made four lines and rolled up one of his fifty pound notes and we sniffed two each and then I didn't feel so tired. He kissed me and it wasn't like kissing a customer, I had real feeling, and we went to the bedroom and we made love. Actually we made love several times and then I went to sleep in his arms. He had to leave early in the morning because he said he had something to do. He left some cocaine for me and said it might help me work or I could sell it to a customer. It was funny because when he left I realised that I had done FFF which I always said that I would never do. Though I suppose actually I did have sex for cocaine so really I did FFC.

Yesterday a customer booked me for two hours with Dao and I went to her apartment. When I first met Dao I thought she was a quiet innocent young girl but now she is so crazy. She was drinking Thai whiskey and as soon as the customer came she was kissing him on the lips and rubbing his groin before he had even paid his money. That is not professional because sometimes customers come with not enough money and sometimes with no money at all. She knelt down and gave him oral and I asked him for the £300 and it was funny because he took out his wallet and paid me while Dao was giving him oral.

Then we went into the bedroom and before I could do anything she had put a condom on him and was having sex with him. He came really quickly and I realised that actually she is not that crazy. The customer had been in the apartment for just ten minutes and already he had come. Then we gave him a massage for an hour and a half and then I gave him oral and I had sex with him while Dao kissed him. It was only after he had gone that we realised we didn't even know his name.

I showered in Dao's bathroom. My itch has stopped and I have no discharge which is good and it means the medicine worked. I am so happy that I didn't have anything serious. The doctor said that Chlamydia is quite common and that a lot of girls have it without even knowing they have it.

As I was walking back to my apartment Oliver phoned me to tell me that I had an hour incall at a flat in Battersea and that the customer wanted to see me straight away. I ordered an Uber taxi. The driver kept looking at me in the mirror and he asked me where I was from and I said Malaysia because I didn't want him to know that I was from Thailand. He said that I looked like I was Thai but I said no I wasn't. He said he had once had a Thai wife but that she had stolen all his money. He said he had met her in Pattaya and he had built a house for her in Korat and that she had said that she was pregnant but it was all a lie and that actually she already had a Thai husband. He started saying horrible things about Thai girls, that they were all liars and that all they cared about is money, and I was so angry but I didn't say anything. Actually I thought it was his own fault. He was fat and bald and ugly and he said that his wife was young and pretty. Why would he think that a young pretty girl would love him? Of course all she wanted was his money. What else did he have to offer? Nothing. I think it serves him right. We Thais have an expression – Som Naam Naa. It means serves you right. It was his own fault. I gave him one star when the ride was over. Reviews are as important to Uber drivers as they are to escorts.

The customer's name was Richard and he was English and quite nice but he kept wanting to do anal. I said that I didn't do anal and he said that when he had booked me he had been told that I did. I said that was wrong and that if he wanted I would give him his money back and he could get another girl but he said no, he wanted me because I was so pretty so we had sex and I pretended to come and that made him happy.

As soon as I got home Oliver phoned me and said that I had a ninety minutes incall and that his name was Luke. Actually I had seen Luke before. He liked to make love many times and I was tired already. After he had sex with me the second time I went into the bathroom and took some of Vince's cocaine to give me energy and then I had sex with Luke again. In ninety minutes he came three times and he wasn't taking Viagra, I am sure. Before I did this job I would never think about taking cocaine but now I understand that it can make the job a bit easier. Customers don't like it when a girl is tired or has no energy.

I had four more customers during the evening, all incall. By the time I went to sleep I had used all the cocaine that Vince had left me and my heart was beating really fast but I am sure that all my customers were really happy because I had £250 in tips!

Chapter 73

Thursday July 2. I wanted to go study online yesterday but I woke up too late and my head hurt like I had a hangover even though I hadn't been drinking. I didn't know that cocaine could give you a hangover! Actually I didn't wake up until one o'clock in the afternoon and that was because Oliver was ringing to tell me that I had an incall booking for two o'clock. I didn't feel like working because I was so tired and I had a headache and I wanted some cocaine to give me some energy but I didn't have any so I made myself as cup of coffee instead.

The customer was called Wolf and he was from Germany. I asked him if Wolf was his name or his nickname and he said that his name was really Wolfgang but everyone called him Wolf. I laughed and said that he was the first Wolf who had ever fucked me and he laughed. He was very good at sex and after half an hour he said he wanted to book me for an extra hour and I called Oliver and he said it was okay but that I had another incall booking for four o'clock. Wolf made love to me four times and I was a bit sore and I only had time for a quick shower before the next customer rang the bell. He said his name was Adam. He was wearing a suit and he kept talking to people about apartments so I think he was an estate agent. He didn't smell very fresh so I had a bubble bath with him and made sure I used lots of shower gel.

As soon as Adam went I phoned Oliver and Oliver said that Robert had booked me for four hours starting at nine o'clock and that made me really happy because I enjoy being with Robert and it is easy money.

I fell asleep on the sofa while I was watching a Netflix movie but then Oliver rang me to say I had another booking.The incall booking was an old man in a suit with a briefcase who didn't say anything to me. When I opened the door he handed me my money and went into the bathroom and showered and then he came out and lay first down on the bed while I gave him a massage and then he turned over and I gave him oral and then I got on top of him and then he came and then he went into the bathroom and showered again and then he dressed and left. He said not one word. And he didn't even smile at me. You know, I think it would be better for him if he saved his money and took care of himself.

After he had gone I lay down on the sofa again to get some sleep and the phone rang and it was Nancy. She was asking how busy I was and I told her very busy and she said that she was very busy, too. In fact she said that all the girls were busy. She didn't know why. Maybe it was because there was no sport on the television and it was a cold day, I said. But she was right. It was a very busy day. It wasn't the evening yet but I had been working for four hours already and I had four hours booked with Robert. Eight hours in one day is a lot, though at least I don't have to have sex with Robert. Actually, time with Robert is quite relaxing, though sometimes it does tickle when he licks my feet.

I had just fallen asleep when the phone rang again. It was Oliver. I had another incall booking, this time for an hour and a half, and the customer wanted me to wear my nurse's uniform.

Before I went to see Robert I phoned Vince and asked him if I could have some more cocaine. I was so tired that I was sure I would fall asleep and I didn't want Robert to think that I was bored with him. Vince said he would bring some around and he did and then he asked me for £200. I was a bit surprised because I thought he would give it to me but of course it is his business so I paid him. If he did give me free cocaine it would be like a working girl doing FFF, I suppose.

When I went to see Robert he asked me if I was okay because I looked tired and I said I was fine. Then he took me into the kitchen and gave me a peanut butter sandwich and a chocolate milkshake and then we went into the bathroom and he gave me a bath and then he carried me into the bedroom and licked my feet and played with himself. I wish all my customers were as good to me as Robert.

I got home at half past one and then Oliver rang me to say that I had another one hour incall. I was so, so, tired and the customer was a bit rough and had been drinking a lot but I just closed my eyes and thought about all the money I was making.

Chapter 74

Friday July 3. I was very busy again yesterday. I don't know why but it is good because I am earning a lot of money. I am so busy that I have had no time to do laundry so I put twelve towels in a black rubbish bag and took them to a laundry. The woman who took them was from Poland, I think, and she frowned when she saw so many towels. I just smiled and didn't say anything. I had a lot of bills to pay, too. I had my electricity bill which is quite high because of all the hot water I use and my council tax bill which I have to pay every month. Just living is expensive. Say you want a bottle of water. In Thailand you can go to a minimart or a 7-11 and bottle of water will cost twelve baht which is less than 20p. But in London a bottle of water costs £1. A Kentucky Fried Chicken meal in Thailand costs about £4 and they will deliver to your house. In London it will cost twice that. And you know, if you eat KFC in Thailand they give you a metal knife and fork and real plate. Some things are much better in Thailand. But not the money that people earn. In London people get a minimum wage which I thinks is about £8 an hour. That is about 320 baht. But in Thailand people working in the fast food industry earn 300 baht a day. Can you believe that?

While I was in the post office paying my council tax, Oliver phoned me to tell me that I had a customer at eleven o'clock for one hour's incall. I hurried back and got ready. The customer was called Ray and he was very nice. He was about fifty I think and had long hair and he could speak some Thai. He said that he liked Thailand and Thai people so I was happy to tell him that I was Thai. I gave him my phone number and said that I would like to see him again, which is true.

After Ray left, Oliver phoned me and said that I had two bookings, one after the other, and then when the second one had gone he called me again and said that I had another booking, this one for half an hour's incall. I had never done half an hour incall before but he said it was okay and that I could charge £100 and that his share would be

£35. Actually I was not happy with half an hour but I did not want to argue with him. The customer was not very nice and he smelled bad but he said that he didn't want to shower because he didn't want to waste time so I had to make love to him and it was really bad.

I don't understand why Oliver gave me a half hour booking. The website says one hour is the minimum unless something has changed. I phoned Nancy and she said that Oliver had given her two half-hour bookings and she wasn't happy either because seeing a customer for half hour is actually hard work. With an hour you can relax but with half an hour you are just trying to make the customer come. She said that we should speak to Oliver on Sunday night and I said that was a good idea.

I slept for a little bit in the evening but then Oliver phoned me and I had an hour's incall followed by half an hour's incall followed by another hour.

Then Candy phoned me and asked if I was busy and I said yes, I was almost too busy and she said that all the girls were. In one way it is good because we are earning a lot of money but in another way it is not so good because I do not have the time to even shower properly. And I am so tired that when the last customer goes all I can do is sleep.

Simon called me and said that he had tried to book me but that Oliver had said that I was busy and I said yes, I was very busy. Actually, I would rather do three hours incall with Simon than see three separate customers. With Simon I get to watch a movie and eat and cuddle and just have sex once. But with three customers I have to have sex with three men. I told Simon that next time he should book me early and he said that he would.

The last customer left at three o'clock in the morning. All my towels were wet and I had run out of toilet rolls and shampoo. I phoned Ice and told him how much I missed him but then I had to stop talking because I missed him so much that I felt my eyes fill with tears. I fell asleep wearing my suspenders and stockings because I was so tired.

Chapter 75

Sunday July 5. I was very busy on Friday and Saturday, and now I know why and I am so angry but I don't know what I can do about it. I had five incalls during the day on Friday and three of them were just for half an hour. Then Simon booked me for three hours from eight o'clock until eleven and he bought me some Chinese food and we watched Netflix movies. I chose Déjà Vu which has Denzel Washington in it. It was a movie about seeing into the future. I wish I could see into my future. I was so tired that I fell asleep while I was watching the movie. When I woke up Simon said that he didn't mind and I felt a bit sad for him because he had paid a lot of money and all I had done was eat his food and sleep. I told him that I was so busy and it was making me tired and he said not to worry. Actually I should have phoned Vince and bought some cocaine because when I take cocaine I have lots of energy.

Simon left at eleven o'clock and then my phone rang. It was Moon, one of the A1 agency girls. She said she had seen my picture and I thought she meant on the agency's website but she didn't. She had seen my picture in a telephone box. I was so shocked and I asked her what she meant. She said that some working girls advertise with cards in phone boxes. The cards have a picture and a phone number and say what the girl will do. Moon said that my card said I would do 'A levels' which is anal and 'O levels' which is oral. I said that was not true and that I never did anal but Moon said she was sure it was me and she described the stockings I was wearing in the picture and I am sure it is one of the photographs from Oliver's website.

Moon said that the girls who advertised in phone boxes weren't as high-class as agency girls. Their customers were cheap and walked around the streets looking for sex and no one knew who they were. She said that she knew a girl who worked in a flat near Oxford Circus and she advertised in phone boxes and she sometimes saw more than twenty customers a day. Customers could pay just £30 for oral and £50 for sex if they were really quick. Moon said yes, you could make good money that way, but you were sure to get sick because it is not good to make love to so many men.

I just sat there shocked because now I know what Oliver is doing. He is advertising me in phone boxes. That is not fair. When I joined the agency he told me that he knew who his customers were and that his customers were all high-class rich men who wanted to spend time with a pretty young girl. But now he is sending me low-class customers who have been walking around the street looking for sex.

I didn't tell Moon that because I was shy. I said that maybe someone had stolen my photograph and Moon said yes, sometimes people did that. If a girl wasn't pretty then she wouldn't get any customers but if she used a photograph of a pretty girl then the customer would come and hopefully not change his mind when he saw it was a different girl. Actually some of the agencies do the same thing but it is not a good idea because if a customer is paying £150 or more for a girl then he should get what he is paying for.

I tried to smile but inside I was so upset that I felt like crying. I asked Moon if she knew what had happened to Bee and Moon said that she had been robbed and killed. The man who had killed her had taken all her money and her jewellery and the police didn't know who it was but thought it was maybe the man who had been stealing from working girls in London. I said that Bee didn't have CCTV at her flat.

On Saturday I went to Oxford Circus and walked around looking in phone boxes. There were a lot of cards advertising all sorts of working girls. There were Asian girls and black girls and Japanese girls and farang girls too. I saw my photograph on a lot of phone boxes. And I saw Nancy and Sandra and Candy and Alice as well. My photograph had a black strip across my eyes but you could tell it was me. And it did say that I did A levels which is not true. Nancy's card said 'Does All Services' and Candy's card had a picture of her in her domination outfit. The number on the cards wasn't the number that Oliver uses on the website. I took some of the cards and then I went to see Nancy. I showed her the card with her photograph on and she was so angry. Chris was there and he was angry too and said that we should stop working for Oliver because he was just a pimp.

Nancy said that we should talk to the other girls and that we could all talk to Oliver on Sunday night and I thought that was a good idea. I gave her the card with Sandra's photograph on it and said she should tell Sandra because I think Sandra is still angry with me and I went to see Candy. Candy was angry and she said she would go and tell Alice and then my phone rang and it was Oliver to say that I had an incall booking. I wanted to tell Oliver that I knew that he had been lying to us but I didn't because it would be better if all the girls were there at the same time.

I was very, very busy on Saturday. I had nine customers and they all wanted sex. By five o'clock I was so tired that I could hardly keep my eyes open so I phoned Vince and bought some cocaine off him. I wanted to tell Vince what had happened but I didn't have time because my next customer was due. I am so angry at Oliver but we can get it sorted out on Sunday night. Then we can all tell him that he is not being fair.

Chapter 76

Monday July 6. My life feels like a nightmare but I know it is not a nightmare, it is real and I won't wake up and find that it's all a dream. I don't know how this has happened but I have a big problem now and I think it is a problem without a solution. I have spent all day crying. Except when I have a customer, then I have to pretend to be happy but inside I am sad, sad, sad. And I am scared, more scared than I have ever been in my life.

I had spoken to Dao and Nancy and Candy and Nancy spoke to Sandra and Vicky and Rachel and Candy told Alice what Oliver was doing and we all agreed that on Sunday night we would go to the Sloane Square flat and talk to Oliver and tell him that we didn't want our pictures in phone boxes.

Then on Sunday morning Cat phoned me and said that I wasn't to go to the Sloane Square flat and that someone would come around to collect the money. I asked why and she sounded a bit angry and said that was what was going to happen and I shouldn't argue. I asked who would be coming to my flat and she said Sacha, the man we had seen at the flat last week. She said Sacha would be coming to the flat at seven o'clock and that he would explain things to me and that I was to give my money to him. I said that I wanted to speak to Oliver and she said that Oliver wasn't there. And she said I had an hour incall at mid-day so I should get ready. The incall customer was called Karl and he was from South Africa and he was quite funny but I didn't enjoy myself because I was so worried about what was happening. After he left I phoned Oliver to say that he had gone but Cat answered the phone. I asked her if I could speak to Oliver and she said that he wasn't there and she sounded upset. I asked her what was wrong but she wouldn't say.

She ended the call and right away Nancy phoned me to ask her why we weren't going to the Sloane Square flat and I said I didn't know and she said she was a bit scared and I said that I was too. She said that

Cat had said that Sacha would be coming to see her about seven-thirty which means that he was coming to see me first. Nancy said she had spoken to Sandra and Sacha was going to her flat at six o'clock. So what was happening was that Sacha was going around to all the flats to collect the money from the girls. Nancy said she wanted to go to the Sloane Square flat because it was fun and we could all eat and talk and play cards and I said I agreed, it was good that all the girls get together. I said I didn't know why Oliver has changed his plan. Before it was a good plan and I didn't like Sacha and I didn't like being told to stay at home like I was a child.

Then I got a call from Cat saying that I had a half hour incall in ten minutes so I had to get ready. The customer was horrible. He smelled of alcohol and cigarettes and had bad skin and he said he didn't want to take a shower because he didn't have time. He was rough and he bit me on my shoulder and I hated having sex with him.

In the afternoon Simon called me to see if I was okay and I wanted to tell him what had happened but I couldn't. I just said that I was a bit tired. He said he would book me for three hours and he would come around to the flat and I could just go to sleep and he would watch television which was so sweet of him. I said okay but that I would probably be busy at about seven o'clock. Simon said no problem and that he would call the agency.

I phoned Oliver's number again and Cat answered and I could tell that she was crying and she said that I shouldn't call her and that Sacha would explain everything and then someone took the phone off her and it was a man and he wanted to know who I was and I just ended the call. I was shaking and angry and upset and I wished I had someone to talk to but I didn't.

At two o'clock my phone rang and it was Oliver's number but it wasn't Oliver and it wasn't Cat, it was a woman who spoke with what sounded like a Russian accent. She said that I had a customer for two-thirty and that his name was Paul and that he wanted me to wear school uniform. I asked her who she was and she said that her name was Natalie and I asked her where Cat was and she said that Cat had gone home and then I asked her where Oliver was and she said that Oliver didn't work for the agency any more and then I was a bit scared because the agency was Oliver's. He set it up, it was his agency, and he ran it. I don't think he would just go away and give it to someone else. Then Natalie said she was too busy to talk to me and she ended the call.

I phoned Nancy and she said that she had spoken to Natalie too and that she agreed that something was wrong. We couldn't talk for long because she had a customer and I was really busy all afternoon and I was so tired that I could hardly keep my eyes open. I phoned Vince and asked him to bring me some cocaine and he did and I paid him £200. He asked me if I was okay and I said I was even though I wasn't. I wanted to see what Sacha had to say before I told anyone else.

I had a customer come at six for an hour. It was Richard, the man who wears his tracksuit and pretends to be out running so that his wife won't know what he is doing. Richard could tell that I wasn't happy but I pretended to smile. I had taken some of Vince's cocaine so I had plenty of energy but the cocaine didn't make me happy.

About five minutes after Richard had left there was a knock at my door. I didn't open it because I only open the door if I have seen who it is on the CCTV at the entrance to the building and then I buzz them in. I didn't know who was at my door but then he knocked again, really hard, and shouted that it was Sacha and that I should open the door. I did. He was wearing a big black coat and behind him were two men that I hadn't seen before who were also wearing big black coats. I was so scared that my legs started to shake. Sacha pushed past me and went into my flat and I went after him.

Sacha said the two men worked for him and that sometimes they would be collecting my money now. Their names were Yuri and Sergey. He said I had to do everything they said, that they spoke with his voice. He asked me where my book was and I got it from the kitchen. He sat down on the sofa and put his feet on the coffee table and looked through the book. Yuri and Sergey kept staring at me and one of them said something and I didn't understand because he spoke in Russian but I am sure that he was talking about my breasts because that's what they were looking at. I went into the bedroom and got my bathrobe and put it on.

Sacha told me to get my money and I did. It was in an envelope and he counted it. I had earned £4,800 during the week so I had to give Oliver £1,600. When he had finished counting it, Sacha said that the agency was now charging fifty per cent commission which meant that

I had to give him £800 more. I said that Oliver only took one third and he said that Oliver wasn't running the agency any more. He said that the agency was now getting me more work so that I should pay them more. I said that wasn't fair. And I said that it wasn't fair that he was putting my photographs in phone boxes. Sacha said something to Yuri and he stepped forward and hit me. Really, I am serious, he slapped my face. No one has ever hit me before, not even my mother or father. My teachers at school in Udon Thani sometimes threatened to smack me if I was naughty but they never did. But this man slapped my face so hard that I started crying.

I ran into the bedroom and tried to close the door but Sacha pushed it open. I ran around the bed and tried to hide but of course there was nowhere to hide. Sacha pointed his finger at me and said that things had changed and that now it was his agency. He said he would pay me fifty per cent and that if I ever argued with him again he would really hurt me.

I was really crying and I said I wanted to go home and I meant Thailand. He said that I couldn't go home because he had my passport. And he said that if I ran away or complained to anyone, he would send people to hurt me in Thailand. He said they would slash my face with a razor so that no man would ever want to look at me again. And he said he knew about my son and he would hurt my son and my mother and my father. He said he knew where I lived in Thailand because he had my ID card and no matter where I went he would be able to find me. He said he would cut me and burn down my house and throw my son into the flames. Really, he said that.

I was crying so hard and my whole body was shaking. He asked me if I understood and I said that I did. He said that if I was a good girl I would still make a lot of money. I asked him when I could go home and he said when I had earned enough money for him and I asked when that would be and he said that he would tell me. Then he told me to get his money and I went into the sitting room and got him £800 from under the carpet.

Yuri said something and Sacha laughed. He said that Yuri wanted a blow job and that I should give him one. I was so scared that I just did what Sacha said. I knelt down in front of him and he opened his trousers and I gave him oral sex until he came in my mouth. I felt sick.

After he came he pushed me back and I fell on the floor and curled up into a ball and cried.

Sacha loaned over me and said that in future Yuri or Sergey would come around every day to collect the money for the agency. Every day I had to give them half of what I earned. He asked me if I understood and I said yes, I did. He patted me on the head and said that I was a good girl and then they all went. They were laughing and I hated them so much that if I had had a gun I would have killed them.

I lay on the floor for a long time crying and then I phoned Nancy but her phone was switched off and I called Dao but her phone kept ringing and she didn't answer.

Then Natalie phoned and said that I had a customer for half an hour incall and that the customer would be around in five minutes. I said that I was sick and couldn't work. She said that I had to work. She said that if I didn't work Sacha would send someone around to the flat to make sure that I did work. She sounded nasty and I knew what she meant. She meant that if I did not work they would hurt me. They would hurt me a lot. So I took some cocaine and then I showered and got ready for the customer.

I kept hoping that Natalie would phone to say that Simon had booked me so that at least I could spend time with a friend but every time she phoned it was to say that I had another customer. In the evening I had seven customers, three for one hour and four for thirty minutes. Before Sunday was always a quiet day and none of us worked on Sunday evening because we went to the Sloane Square flat. But now Sunday is like every other day and it is busy. So busy that if I did not have the cocaine to help me I think I would have collapsed.

I hate this job now. I hate it more than anything. But I don't know what I can do to save myself.

Chapter 77

Wednesday July 8. What is happening to me is not fair. All I ever wanted to do was to work and make good money to take care of my son and my family. But now I feel like a prisoner because I have to work for Sacha. And it is not just Sacha, I think. I think now the mafia are running the agency. Russian Mafia. Oliver has gone now and so has Cat and it is always the girl called Natalie who calls and tells us who our customers are. Work is horrible now. Really horrible. When Oliver was the boss I saw a few customers a day and they were usually nice and kind and I had a good time but now I don't like most of the men who come to see me. A lot come for just half an hour and all they want is oral and sex and they don't want to talk to me or get to know me. Some of them ask for anal and I say that I don't do anal and some of them get angry because it says I do A Levels on my card. It's like before I was an escort and now I am just a prostitute and I feel dirty. I know now that there is nothing I can do to stop what is happening. I know that for sure if I do not do what Sacha says he will hurt me and he will hurt my family.

On Monday morning I went to see Nancy. Chris was there and he was very angry. Nancy was crying and said that Sacha had told her what he told me. No one had slapped Nancy but they had told her that they knew where her mother lived and that if she tried to run away someone in Thailand would go and kill her mother. They knew Nancy's mother's address and everything about her. I believe that they have someone in Thailand who knows all about us now. Nancy said she was scared and I said I was scared too. She said she was working very hard now and seeing more then ten customers every day and she didn't want to because she wanted to spend more time with Chris.

Chris wanted to go to the police but Nancy said that the British police wouldn't be able to protect her family in Thailand which I think is true. Chris said the British police could talk to the Thai police but we told Chris that he didn't understand what life was like in Thailand.

If somebody wanted to hurt our families they could. Chris said that he would talk to Sacha and see if he could get him to let Nancy go. He said he would tell the newspapers about what was happening and that Sacha wouldn't want the newspapers to know so maybe he would agree to Nancy leaving the agency. I didn't think Sacha would listen to anyone but I didn't say anything to Chris.

Then my phone rang and it was Natalie telling me I had a customer so I had to go home. On Monday night Sacha came to see me and he looked at my book and then took half the money I had earned. I had seen six customers who came for half an hour each so that was £600 and I had four customers for one hour which was another £600 so I had earned £1,200 and so Sacha took £600. That means I had £600 for myself which sounds like a lot but I had to have sex with ten men for that which means I was getting only £60 each time which is not good.

I was tired and I was sore and all I wanted to do was to sleep. I told Sacha I wanted to stop work and he said I couldn't. I said that wasn't fair and he said he didn't care what was fair. He took a flick-knife out of his pocket and showed it to me and he said he would cut my face if I tried to stop working. I asked him if I could pay him money to stop working and he laughed. He said a good whore could earn him £200,000 in a year so if I wanted to stop working I had to pay him £200,000 which is a fortune. Sacha said once I had earned £200,000 for him he would let me go but I don't believe him.

I knew there was no point in saying anything to him so I just stayed quiet. He laughed and then he took a photograph out of his pocket and showed it to me and it was Ice with my mother in front of my house and I knew then that I was trapped and there is nothing I can do to save myself. I belong to Sacha now like a cow belongs to a farmer. I don't know why this has happened to me because I am a good person and I never do anything to hurt anybody.

I went to sleep after Sacha went but I was woken up by Nancy who was crying so much that I couldn't understand what was wrong so I had to go around to her flat to talk to her. She was crying and crying and wouldn't stop but eventually she told me what had happened. Chris had been in the flat when Sacha went to get his money and Chris said that he didn't want Nancy to work any more. Sacha had smiled and nodded and said that he understood. Sacha said that he would let Nancy leave the agency and then he held out his hand to shake and

Chris took his hand and then Sacha headbutted him. He broke Chris's nose and then he kicked him between the legs and Chris fell down. Then Sacha picked up a lamp and smashed that onto Chris's head and then he started stamping on his legs so hard that he broke the bones and then he kicked him in the stomach many times. Nancy tried to help but Sacha punched her and she collapsed. Then Sacha kept kicking Chris until he was unconscious. Then Nancy said that Sacha phoned his friends and they came and took Chris away. Now Nancy doesn't know if Chris is alive or dead. And Sacha told her that if she ever told anybody what had happened he would do the same to her and then he would do the same to her mother.

Nancy hugged me and said she was so scared and I said that I was scared too. It is like Sacha is not scared of anything or anybody and can do whatever he likes to other people. Nancy said she wanted to kill herself and I understood how she felt but I said no, she mustn't do that. She said that being dead would be better than the way she was living now and I think she might be right. We lay together on her bed and cried together and that's what we did all night.

I was busy on Tuesday, too. It was like I had a constant stream of customers one after the other. Sometimes I didn't even have time to wash or shower. Every one of the customers I saw was a new customer and I asked some of them where they had heard about me and they all said they had seen my picture in a phone box. And you know, they had seen my pictures all over London not just near my flat. Not one of the customers had come because they had seen the agency website. Now I know what I am. I am not an escort any more. I am a prostitute. That is not what I wanted but now it is my life. I am so sad. Sad, sad, sad.

I want to phone Ice and see his face and hear his voice but I can not because I know I will just start crying and I do not want to upset him.

At about six o'clock my phone rang and it was Robert. He asked me if I was okay and I lied and said that I was. He said that he had tried to book me three times but that each time he had been told that I was busy. I said I was busy but I asked him if he would keep trying and he said that he would. I said that I missed him which was true.

At about midnight I phoned Dao to see if she was okay and you know, she said she was happy with the way she was working. She said she was really busy and earning very good money and that really it was fair that she gave half to Sacha because they were getting her more money than Oliver did. I asked her if Sacha had threatened her and she said he had but that there was no need for him to threaten her because she was happy. And she said that Sacha was quite cute and that she had had sex with him for free when he went to her flat. I couldn't believe what she was saying. She did FFF with the man who is threatening to kill my son. I think there is something wrong with Dao. I think she is a bit crazy.

Sacha came to get my money at two o'clock in the morning. He checked my book and I gave him £750 and he asked me if everything was okay and I smiled and said it was. After he went I cried and cried. Then I got a text from Robert saying that he missed me and that made me smile a bit. I sent him a text back saying that I missed him. Maybe Robert can help me. He is rich and rich people have power. That is true in Thailand and it is true in England, too. But I am a bit scared that if I ask Robert for help and Sacha finds out then Sacha might do something bad to him, and to me. I don't think Sacha is scared of anybody. And even if Robert helps me, how will I be able to protect my family?

Chapter 78

Thursday July 9. It seems like all I do now is work and sleep, work and sleep, and sometimes I eat. I am so tired, so tired that my life feels like a dream. Sometimes when I am having sex it feels like it is someone else on the bed, not me. If it wasn't for the cocaine that I buy from Vince I wouldn't be able to do it. Actually I am making quite a bit of money even though I have to give half to Sacha. I am much busier than before. Much, much busier. And I am saving money because I have no time to go shopping and I did not play cards on Sunday night. But that does not mean I am happy because I am not happy. I hate my life now.

Most of my jobs are incall and a lot of them are for thirty minutes. I understand why. It is because Sacha wants to make as much money from me as possible. If I do one hour incall then I charge £150. When Oliver was in charge, I would keep £100 and give £50 to Oliver. Now I keep £75 and I give £75 to Sacha. But if I see two customers for half an hour each, then I earn £200 and I keep £100 and give £100 to Sacha. That means that I earn the same but Sacha earns £25 more. But what is not fair is that now I am having to work twice as hard as I worked before. Before I could have sex with one man to earn £100 but now I have to have sex with two men. I am working twice as hard.

Outcalls are still for one hour. It would be impossible to do outcall for just thirty minutes. Outcall means travelling to where the customer is so that will cost money and take time. If I do an hour's outcall then I charge £210 and now I keep £105 and I give £105 to Sacha. But I have to pay for my taxi and not all my outcall customers tip me so if I have to pay for my taxi then I earn less for outcall then incall but Sacha gets more. Before when I did an hours outcall I would keep £140 and Oliver would get £70 so now outcall is not such a good deal for me. But I prefer outcall because it means I am not so rushed. I can relax a bit. When I am in my room seeing customers for half an hour then I am not relaxed.

At about five o'clock Natalie phoned me and said that I had to do two hours incall with Sandra at her flat. I didn't want to do it because I know that Sandra is still not happy with me but I know that I can not argue with Natalie because if I do she will tell Sacha and then I will be in trouble.

I got to the flat just before the customer was due because I didn't want to talk to Sandra but actually she was okay and quite sweet to me. I asked her what she thought about Sacha and she said she wasn't happy. She said her boyfriend was not happy and I told her what had happened to Nancy's boyfriend Chris. Nancy had phoned me to tell me that she had gone to see Chris in hospital and that he was really hurt. The doctors had asked him what had happened and he told them that he had fallen downstairs. He said that if he told them what had really happened then Sacha would kill him and kill Nancy. Sandra said she didn't think Sacha would kill them but I told her that he had said he would cut me with a knife and that he would kill my son. He has our passports and our ID cards and he knows where we live.

Sandra said it would not be a problem to get a new passport because all we had to do was to go to the Thai Embassy in London and tell them who we were. And it would be easy to get a ticket and go back to Thailand. We could say that we had visas in the passports that were stolen so we wouldn't have a problem leaving the country. I said that maybe Sacha did have friends in Thailand and that if he did then he could still hurt us. Sandra said that when we got to Thailand we could change our names and get new ID cards because it is easy to change your name in Thailand. But I am not sure if that would work. I think Sacha is a very bad man who is not scared of anybody and I think that if we run away and he finds us then really he will hurt us a lot and maybe kill us. I have never met anyone as evil as Sacha.

The customer's name was Owen and he was English but not from London. He was from a city called Newcastle which is up near Scotland and he had a strange accent that I could hardly understand. I think he had taken Viagra because he had a red face and sniffed a lot and he stayed hard for the whole two hours. Sandra gave him oral and then I gave him oral and then he had sex with Sandra from behind and then I went on top and then he wanted oral from me while he kissed Sandra and then he made love to me doggy-style and then he wanted me to lick him while he had sex with Sandra. He made love for the whole two hours and I was exhausted. After Owen had gone I went home without showering because I wanted to get away from Sandra. I don't think she has a good heart and I do not think I can trust her. I wanted to talk to Vince but when I called him his phone was off. I left a message saying that I wanted to talk to him and that I needed to buy some more cocaine.

I had five more customers after I got home and the last one left at three o'clock in the morning. Three of them asked for anal and I had to tell them that I do not do anal. When Natalie phoned me I asked her to change what was written on my cards because so many customers want me to do anal and she said I should do it and charge more but I said I didn't want to do it so she said she would talk to Sacha which was nice of her. When I had finished work I was so tired that I did not even shower I just fell asleep on the sofa.

I woke up when there was a banging on the door and it was Sacha coming to collect his money. I gave him £750 and he went. He didn't say anything about anal so maybe Natalie hadn't spoken to him. I went into the bedroom and fell asleep right away. I had bad dreams all night and in them Bee was covered in blood and shouting at me that I should run, run, run because I was going to die if I stayed where I was. I want to run, really I do, but I don't know where I can run to where I will be safe.

Chapter 79

Friday July 10. I wish I was dead. Really. My life now is horrible and I don't think there is anything I can do to make it better. I have to do whatever Sacha says and if I don't he will hurt me and my family. I want to run but there is nowhere I can run to.

They came to my flat at eleven o'clock in the morning. It was Yuri and Sergey. Yuri did all the talking while Sergey just stared at me and grinned like it made him happy to see me cry.

Yuri said that customers had complained that I did not do anal. I said that I never did anal, I would do anything else and I would give good service but I did not do anal. Yuri said that anal was nothing, I was a whore and whores did whatever their customers wanted them to. I said no, I wasn't a whore, I was an escort, and escorts could choose what they did.

He shook his head and said that I was not an escort, I was a whore. If a customer wanted my mouth, I had to give him my mouth. If a customer wanted my pussy then I had to give them my pussy. If a customer wanted my arse then I had to give him my arse. I was a whore and I had no choice. I was so unhappy that I could not speak, I just stood there shaking my head.

What happened then is so horrible I do not want to talk about it. I do not want to think about it. Sergey said something in his language to Yuri and they both laughed and then Yuri grabbed me and took me into the bedroom and they both took off my clothes. I tried to scream but he used the belt of my robe to tie my mouth and then they threw me on the bed and they both did anal to me. Both of them did it and do you know what, they did not even use a condom. They were so rough and the pain was so bad that I nearly passed out. They were cursing me and saying that if I ever complained about anal then next time five men would come and they would rape me all night. They said I was their whore and I must never ever argue with them again.

When they had finished they left me on the bed and I just lay there crying and then after fifteen minutes Natalie rang and said I had an incall customer. I went to the bathroom and when I washed myself there was blood. Quite a lot of blood, actually.

The first customer was okay. He was a businessman in his forties, I think, and he only wanted oral. But then I was busy all day. I had twelve customers. Three of them wanted anal and I did it. I just lay there and let them do it to me. It hurt a lot because Sacha's men had been so rough but I did not cry, I just lay there and tried to imagine that I was somewhere else and that it was happening to somebody else. I tried to feel like a block of wood because nothing can hurt a block of wood.

After the first customer went Vince phoned me and said he was sorry but his phone battery had died last night and I said I need some cocaine and he brought some for me and I gave him £200. Using cocaine is the only way I can get through the day now. It gives me energy. I wanted to tell Vince about what had happened to my life but I don't think he can help me so I didn't. I don't think anyone can help me now. I feel so alone and sad, sad, sad.

Chapter 80

Sunday July 12. On Saturday I had twelve customers. Seven were for half an hour incall, four were for one hour incall, and one was a three hour incall. Four of the customers wantcd anal. Actually now anal is not too bad. It doesn't hurt if I relax and think about something else and it means I don't have to look at the customer. I try to do it doggy style now too because that means I don't see the customer and I can close my eyes and think about something else. I still make noises as if I enjoy it because otherwise they might complain to Sacha that I am not giving good service, but really I hate every minute.

The outcall job was okay, actually. He was a businessman from Bristol which is in the West Country. His name was George and he was about fifty-five and he was quite gentle. He couldn't get very hard so we didn't make love properly but I gave him a massage and oral and for most of the time we just lay cuddling on his bed. He actually let me go after two hours even though he paid for three.

I needed some toilet rolls and I knew that the Chinese supermarket in Chinatown usually had some so I booked an Uber taxi and went there. When I got out of the taxi I saw Cat coming out of the supermarket with two carrier bags. She was wearing a facemask but it was definitely her. She didn't want to talk to me but I wouldn't go away. She said she didn't want to talk to me but I said that she had to because what had happened to me wasn't fair. I had worked for the agency for more than four months and I had been a good worker. But I had been working for her and Oliver and now I was working for Sacha and that was not fair because I hadn't chosen to work for Sacha.

Cat said it wasn't her fault. Sacha had taken over the agency and there was nothing she could do. I asked her why Oliver had let Sacha take over the agency and Cat laughed and said that there was nothing Oliver could do. Sacha was Russian Mafia and he could kill people. I said I wanted to speak to Oliver and she said I couldn't because she didn't know where he was.

Cat said that Oliver had gone with Sacha and two other men and she hadn't seen him since and his mobile was switched off. I asked her what she thought had happened to Oliver and she said she didn't know. I asked her if she had gone to the police and she said if she went to the police then Sacha would kill her, for sure. Sacha had killed people in Russia, that's what Oliver had told her. He was a gangster who dealt in guns and drugs and prostitutes and he wasn't scared of anything or anybody.

I asked her if she thought that Sacha had killed Oliver and Cat said she didn't think that, but she thought that Oliver was so scared that he had run away. I asked her what she was going to do and she said she was going to bring some Thai girls over from Bangkok and have them work in a flat in Chelsea but that she wouldn't have an internet escort agency again because it was too dangerous. If you were on the internet then anybody could see how many girls you had and know how much money you were making.

Then I asked Cat if Sacha was telling the truth about what he could do to our families in Thailand and she said yes, she was sorry but he had friends who were Russian mafia who worked in Pattaya and that was why he wanted our passports and ID cards. He had sent copies to his friends in Pattaya and they already knew everything about where we lived and who our families were. She said that all I could do was to work for Sacha. She said that I had no choice. Then my phone rang and it was Natalie saying that I had an incall job in fifteen minutes. Cat ran away when I was talking to Natalie. She got into a taxi and drove off and I was so angry but there was nothing I could do. I got a taxi and when I got back to my flat the customer was outside waiting for me.

Yuri came to get my money at three o'clock in the morning. During the day I had earned £1,840 which meant that I had to give him £920. I think Sacha is making a lot of money from us girls, much more than Oliver ever got. There are nine girls working for the agency so if they are all giving him almost £900 a day then every day he is earning about £8,000 every day which means in one year he will earn almost three million pounds. I do not think I will be able to work like this for one year, though. I think I would rather die than do this for a year.

On Saturday Natalie sent me my first customer at eleven o'clock in the morning which meant that I only slept for six hours. I felt terrible but I had some cocaine so I took that so that I had some energy. Natalie sent me three more customers before five o'clock but then it was quiet for three hours so I got some sleep then. But I had to do laundry first. I have so many customers now that I don't have time to give them clean towels any more. If the towels are wet then I put them in the dryer for a bit but if they are not wet I just use them again. Before I used to use a clean towel on the bed for every customer but now I keep the same towel on the bed all day. I don't shower after every customer now. I don't have the time and even if I did then it wouldn't be good for my skin to have ten or twelve showers every day.

You know, before I was an escort girl and I quite liked my job and I was proud that my customers liked me and I gave good service. But now I am a whore and no one cares about me. They just want to use me and that makes me feel bad.

Natalie called me again at eight o'clock and I was busy all night. Nancy called me three times during the night asking me if I would go around to see her but I couldn't because I was so busy. I didn't finish working until three o'clock in the morning and then I went to see her. She was crying and saying that she wished she was dead, and I said that I understood how she felt. Nancy said that she was as busy as me and that one day she had had fifteen customers. She said she hurt inside, too, and sometimes when she went to the toilet there was blood.

I asked her about Chris and she said that Chris had phoned her and told her to stay away from the hospital because the police kept coming to see him to find out what had happened. Nancy said that Chris was very scared of Sacha and said that Nancy had to do whatever Sacha said because otherwise he would hurt Chris again and maybe kill him.

Nancy said that she couldn't sleep she was so worried and that she was going to get some sleeping pills from a doctor. I said that I always fell asleep really quickly because I was so tired but she said she couldn't sleep because she was thinking too much. We both lay on her bed and held each other and cried and eventually we slept. We woke up when her phone rang at ten o'clock in the morning. It was Natalie, telling her to get ready for a customer so I had to leave her and go home.

Chapter 81

Tuesday July 14. I bought more condoms yesterday. Now I use more than a dozen every day, sometimes twenty or more. I had to buy soap powder, too, and shampoo and soap and KY Jelly. I use a lot of KY Jelly now because I do anal three or four times every day. I don't know why English men like anal sex so much but a lot of them do. I have never heard of a Thai man wanting do that. I think they would think it was dirty. The Indian guy had facemasks and he was selling them for £5 each. I bought ten, and some more hand sanitiser. He asked me if I was okay because I didn't look good and I said I was fine, I just needed some sleep.

At two o'clock in the afternoon Natalie phoned me and said I had to go to Dao's apartment to do ninety minutes incall. I had to wait until Dao was free because she already had a customer and I had only been in her flat for five minutes when the new customer came. Dao said it was her fourth customer already that day. She said she has been really busy since Sacha took over the agency and is making more money than she ever dreamed about. She is right. When Oliver ran the agency I made about £300 a day profit, sometimes £400, but now almost every day I make £800 or £900. We are making more money but we are working too hard. My insides hurt all the time now, though it doesn't hurt as much when I take cocaine. And I am so tired when I wake up in the morning. It's like I never get enough sleep. I hardly ever phone Ice any more. I know that he will be able to tell how tired and sad I am and he will ask me when I am going back to Thailand and I don't know what I can tell him. I don't think Sacha will ever let me leave.

I took a bit of cocaine before I went to see Dao and I was glad that I did because the customer wanted lots of sex. He was fairly young, maybe twenty five, and he said that he was a property developer and that he drove a Ferrari and had a big house in Surrey which is where rich people live. I don't think he had taken Viagra but he was very strong and made love to us both in lots and lots of positions. He said he loved Asian girls because they would do anything and I wanted to tell him that I only did anything because Sacha had said that he would hurt me if I said no but I didn't say that.

We used lots of condoms and at one point we ran out and Dao told me to get some more from the drawer by the bed and I did and that was when I got a shock that made me shake. You know what I saw in the drawer? It was the small bottle of perfume that Bee had - the magic perfume that made men fall in love with her. I am sure it was the same bottle because I recognised the Khmer writing on it. I took out the condoms and closed the drawer and then the customer put on a new condom and made love to me. I was a bit scared when I saw the perfume bottle in Dao's drawer because I know that Bee and Dao were not friends so I know that Bee would not have given her the bottle. That means either Dao took it from Bee's flat or someone else took it from her flat, and whoever took it from her flat might have killed Bee.

After the customer left I had a shower and when I came out of the bathroom I was so shocked because I saw Dao taking heroin. She was doing what we Thais call chasing the dragon where you put heroin on a piece of silver paper and heat it with a cigarette lighter and then breath in the smoke. I have never done it, ever. Heroin is a very dangerous drug. Dao said that it helped her relax and that she smoked heroin two or three times a day. She asked me if I wanted some and I said no.

The customer left about fifteen minutes early but we didn't phone Natalie right away, we just relaxed. We don't get much time to relax since Oliver left.

We talked about Nancy because Nancy had phoned Dao to say how unhappy she was and I said yes, she had been crying with me, too. I said that it might be because she was pregnant and Dao was surprised because she didn't know that Nancy was pregnant. I said it was a secret and Dao said that was okay, she wouldn't tell anybody.

Dao said her young sister was coming to work in London. Her name is Tip and she is eighteen years old. Dao said Tip was applying for a student visa and if she got the visa then she could start working for the agency. I was really surprised because I hate the agency and I hate what I have to do but Dao she doesn't seem to mind. I can't believe that she would want her young sister to do this job but she was serious. She said if Tip could get her own visa and didn't need a contract then she could earn a lot of money. In just two months she could earn enough to build her own house. I think there is something wrong with Dao. Maybe it is because she is smoking heroin that she can not think clearly.

Dao closed her eyes and sighed as if she was dreaming. I went into the bedroom and got the perfume bottle from her drawer and when I went back into the main room her eyes were open but she looked a bit dizzy. I asked her where she had gotten it from and she said that Sacha had given it to her and then I knew for sure that Sacha is a very dangerous man because I am sure now that it was him who killed Bee. I couldn't tell Dao what I thought because Dao likes Sacha and does FFF for him which is probably why he gave her the perfume. She said that she liked the smell and that ever since she had been using the perfume, Sacha had been crazy for her.

Now I think I understand everything. I think Sacha killed Bee and stole her money and her perfume and he gave the perfume to Dao and she used it but she didn't know that it is magic and that now Sacha has fallen in love with her. Dao was smiling and giggling and she lay back on the sofa and I asked her if I could borrow the perfume for a while because I thought it smelled lovely and she giggled and said of course I could because I was her best friend and that it was thanks to me that she was doing this job and she was making so much money. I put the bottle in my bag and went home. On the way home Vince called me and asked me if I wanted to buy some cocaine and I said yes, I did. I asked him to come around that evening because now I have more than £10,000 in my apartment and I need his help to send it to my bank account in Udon Thani.

After I got home I had five more customers. One of them was black. His name was Derek and he was from Brixton which is in South London and he spoke just like he was English. He repaired computers and was quite smart and to tell the truth I had quite a good time with him. *Jai Dee* we say in Thai, which means he has a good heart. Not like Sacha and Yuri and Sergey. They are *Jai Dam* and *Jai Lai* and even *Jai Sat*, which are bad words in Thai.

Yuri came to collect my money at half past two in the morning. I had £850 for him. He said that next Saturday night there would be a party at the house in St John's Wood and that all the girls from the agency would be going. He said that Sacha wanted me to do a sex show with Candy and Dao, a domination show with Candy and Dao being the dominant ones and me being the slave. Yuri said he was looking forward to seeing what the girls were going to do to me and he smiled and it was a very cruel smile. I was a bit scared but I know I have no choice. I have to do whatever they say. That is my life now. He told me to give him oral and I did and then he said he wanted to have sex so I went to the bedroom and lay down. He took off his clothes and before I could do anything he was having sex with me. I begged him to use a condom but he wouldn't. When he went I rushed to the bathroom and spent ages washing myself, but no matter how hard I washed I didn't feel clean.

Chapter 82

Wednesday July 15. I can't go on like this for much longer. It is too much. I am working too hard. I am tired all the time and I know that if it was not for the cocaine I am taking then I would not be able to stay awake. Now I have to buy cocaine from Vince every day. That is £200 a day I have to spend.

Last night I went to see Robert. I was so pleased when Natalie called to say that Robert had booked me for three hours outcall. I was very tired when I went to see him because I had already seen six customers but I didn't take cocaine because my time with Robert is always easy time. We went into the kitchen and he made me a peanut butter sandwich and a chocolate milkshake. He asked me if I was okay and I lied and said that I was because I do not want him to know how much trouble I am in. I know that he would want to help me but I think that Sacha is a very dangerous man and I think he might hurt Robert if he thought Robert was a problem. I do not want Robert to be a problem for Sacha because Robert is a really nice man. We went into the bedroom and Robert licked my toes and stroked me and I tried to relax but all I could think about was how terrible my life has become. Before I went home I hugged him tightly and said 'I love you, Daddy' and do you know, actually I think I do love him. I wish he was my Daddy and that he could make everything all right for me but really I do not think anyone can do that for me.

As soon as I got home more customers started to come. One after the other. You know, now I have seen so many customers that I can not remember their faces. Usually I do not even ask them their names now. I do not send any texts any more at night. I am too tired. Some of my regular customers send me texts saying they miss me and asking if I am okay but I don't reply any more.

At two o'clock in the morning Yuri came for his money. I had £850 for him but he said that wasn't enough. I said no, he could check the book and £850 was half of what I had earned. He said that Sacha had decided that we should give him £250 extra every day for the cost of advertising and protection. That was the new rule. I said that wasn't fair and he hit me. Really, he slapped me across the face. He said life wasn't fair and that I was lucky that Sacha let me keep anything because I was just a whore. I didn't cry even though my eyes filled with tears. I just nodded and said okay because there was nothing else I could do and I gave him another £250. Then he told me to give him oral sex and I did. I wanted to bite, bite, bite and hurt him the way he hurt me, but I didn't. I did what he wanted and then he went.

Candy, Nancy and Wanda all called me during the night, crying. They all said that it wasn't fair that Sacha was now taking half of what we earned plus £250 but they all said that they were too scared to do anything. They all said they hated working every day, too. Before we used to have Sundays off but now every day is a busy day. We never get time to relax or have fun, it is just work, work, work, sex, sex, sex. We are all trapped. We are like farm animals now and we have no choice, we have to do what the farmer wants because the farmer has the power of life and death over his animals.

Chapter 83

Thursday July 16. Yesterday was a horrible day. The worst day of my life. I had sixteen customers. The first one came at eleven o'clock in the morning. The last one left at three o'clock the next day. Only one didn't want sex. Five wanted anal. When Yuri came to get my money he wanted oral and I did what he wanted. I don't care any more. It's as if my body doesn't belong to me any more. Now it is as if everything that happens is happening to someone else and I am just watching it.

I am too tired to do any laundry and too tired to clean my apartment. I hardly have time to eat. Most of the time I eat noodles that I buy from a small shop near my apartment. They are like MaMa noodles which I eat in Thailand but they are made in Japan. They don't taste as good as MaMa noodles but I don't care. I haven't eaten watermelon for a long time. I hardly have time to eat when I am working. The customers keep coming, like a flood that I can not stop. Before, when Oliver ran the agency, I would call him after each customer to say that he had finished and then I would wait for him to call me about the next customer. But now Natalie calls all the time to tell me that my customer's time is up and then I have to tell him to go or he has to pay me more money. And then Natalie tells me that I have five minutes or ten minutes before the next customer comes. Sometimes a customer will ring the bell before the old customer has gone so I have to tell him to hurry and once I had to put one customer in the kitchen until the new customer was in the bedroom. I can not complain because if I complain then Natalie will tell Sacha and he will punish me.

After the last customer goes then usually I fall asleep on the sofa, without even showering. I feel dirty all the time. Dirty inside and outside. My insides hurt all the time and I think my itch is back. Sometimes when I go to the toilet there is blood. Not too much but it is blood. I want to go and see a doctor but I don't want to ask Natalie for time off because I know that she will tell Sacha.

When I fell asleep I had bad dreams, and then Bee came to talk to me. She was covered in blood and one of her eyes was half closed and she was crying. I couldn't tell what she was saying to me because she was crying so much. Then she screamed 'Nancy!' and I woke up.

I was shaking because the dream was so real. I phoned Nancy and it took her ages to answer the phone and when she did she sounded really sleepy and I could tell that something was wrong. I asked her what had happened and she was mumbling about Sacha and her baby. I said I'd go to see her and I couldn't hear what she said so I just put on my coat and ran over to her apartment.

I kept pressing her bell but she didn't answer and then I phoned her again and I think she was asleep but she woke up and buzzed me in. I had to bang on the door before she let me into her flat and I could see right away that something bad had happened. She had a bruise on her eye and her chin was red and on the coffee table there was a bottle of sleeping tablets and bottle of Thai whiskey. I asked her what she had done and she was so sleepy she couldn't say anything. I knew what she had done. She had swallowed lots of tablets and whiskey.

I didn't know what to do because she was dying and I couldn't call for an ambulance because they might tell the police and then Nancy would get into trouble. I tried to get her to drink water but she was too sleepy and she lay down on the sofa and curled up into a ball. Then I phoned Vince and he said he would come right round and he did though by the time he got there Nancy was hardly breathing.

Vince said we had to keep her awake so we carried her to the bathroom and we stood under the shower with the water cold and then she woke up a bit. Vince told me to make coffee and while I was in the kitchen he made her sick by pushing his fingers down her throat. She threw up a lot and the bathroom was a mess but Vince said we had to get the tablets out of her stomach because once they were all in her blood then she would die.

We made her drink the coffee and then we kept her walking around and around and talking to her. Vince said she would be okay, he said if she had swallowed Paracetamol then she would have poisoned her liver but sleeping tablets were okay if you got them out of the stomach. After four hours or so Nancy wasn't so sleepy but she was crying a lot.

She said that Sacha had beaten her up and that he had told her that she had to get an abortion. She said that Sacha had found out that she was pregnant and she didn't know how because it was a secret but I know how.

I told Dao and she must have told Sacha so what happened to Nancy was all my fault. She said that Sacha went to her apartment and said that she was a whore and pregnant whores can not work so he would get Natalie to take her to a doctor who would take the baby out. Nancy said that she wanted to keep the baby, but now she had no choice. She started crying again and said that she wanted to die. I told her not to be silly but actually I understood how she felt. I want to die, too.

Vince left us in the morning and I lay on the bed with Nancy, holding her. Then at eleven o'clock in the morning Natalie called my phone and said that I had a customer and I had to go. I took the sleeping tablets and the whiskey with me. When I went Nancy said that she felt better but I felt worse.

The customer wanted anal and he was very rough. I had no condoms but I didn't care, I just lay on the bed and let him do what he wanted to do and thought about Ice and how much I missed him. The customer left without saying anything and I got up and sat on the sofa and cried and cried and cried. I phoned Ice and told him that I loved him but that was all I could say because I was crying so much so I hung up.

So that is it. That is the story of my life so far. Now I know one thing for sure and that is that I can not carry on like this any more. I keep looking at the bottle of perfume that Dao had given me. It is Bee's magic perfume, I know that for sure. Before I thought that maybe Sandra had killed Bee but now I know for sure that it was Sacha because he gave the bottle to Dao. Sacha is not scared of anybody. He is the most dangerous man that I have ever met in my whole life. I do not know why I have ended up in his power. Maybe I did something wrong in a previous life and this is the price I must pay.

I think that maybe what Nancy tried to do was not such a bad idea. At least if you are dead then no one can hurt you. I have Nancy's tablets here and I have counted them. There are thirty-four tablets in the bottle and I think that will be enough for what I want to do.

Sacha will never let me leave. He will never let me go and live with my son in Udon Thani. He will work me until I am dead. I know that for sure now. He wants me to be his slave. We are all his slaves now. No one can help me. I am sure the police can not help me and the Thai Embassy can not help me. Even if I run away Sacha's friends in Thailand will hurt me and my family. There is no escape for me.

There is only one way that I can end this. There is only one way that I can make the pain stop and now I know what I am going to do. Nothing can stop me. I have to do what I have to do. I have decided and nothing now can change my mind. I hope that no one thinks I am a bad girl for what I am about to do. I am not a bad girl. All I ever wanted to do was to help my family and to give them a better life. That is why I did this job in the first place. It is not my fault that everything has gone wrong and my life has been ruined. I am going to end this, once and for all.

EPILOGUE

I did it. I did it and now I am happy, happy, happy. I am living in Udon Thani with my son and my life is perfect. Nancy has gone home, too. She is living with her family in Korat. We flew back to Thailand together. The airport is still closed but the Thai Government is allowing Thai people to fly home on repatriation flights. We had to wear masks on the plane and then when we got to the airport in Bangkok everyone was dressed like they were in a science fiction film in blue overalls and masks and plastic shields over their faces. They took us to buses and drove us to a place that looked like an Army camp and we had to stay in a room on our own for fifteen days. They brought us food on plastic trays and we had to clean our own rooms and they tested us for Covid every week. The test was horrible, they pushed a swab all the way up your nose, so far that you can feel it touch your brain. The quarantine was horrible but I had my phone so I could FaceTime with Ice every day and watch Thai soap operas. After fifteen days they let me and Nancy go. Nobody knows that she was called Nancy in London, of course. In Thailand everyone calls her Noy. She doesn't know what I did to get away from the Russians but I gave her enough money so that she doesn't have to work any more. I hope she stays in Thailand now because she was going crazy in London.

It is August now and nobody is dying of Covid in Thailand. Not many people are dying in London, either. Maybe ten a day. It looks like it is over and everything is going to be okay now. I am so glad.

The only one who knows what I did to get out of London is Candy and she had to know because I needed her help to do what I had to do. I shared the money with her because she helped me. She said she wanted to stay in London. She said she wants to set up her own agency specialising in domination. I think she actually enjoys domination and would do it even if she didn't get paid. That would be DFF, I suppose. Domination For Free. But she isn't going to do it for free. She is going to pay for some contracts for Thai girls and bring them to London and train them to do domination. She is building a dungeon in Chelsea and another dungeon in Canary Wharf, which is where all the banks and stockbrokers are. Candy said that bankers and stockbrokers really like domination.

What I like is what I am doing now. I am spending time with my son who I love more than anything else in the world. He is so happy that I am back and I am happy, too. When I first got home he wouldn't let go of me for the first few days. Everywhere I went he went with me, holding my hand, even when I went to the toilet. It was because he was scared that I would leave him again. My mum and dad were happy that I was back, too, and they had many, many questions for me. Most of the questions I couldn't answer, of course, but I tried not to lie because it is not good to lie to anyone, especially to your mother and father who gave you life.

After Nancy tried to kill herself I kept her sleeping tablets. And I had Bee's perfume that Dao had given me. I wasn't sure that the magic perfume would work but I knew that I had to try. Bee had said that the perfume only worked for a short time after you put it on your skin so I waited until Yuri knocked on my door and then I went into the bathroom and dabbed some on my neck and my breasts and then I opened the door and as soon as I did I hugged him like I hug my regular customers and I kissed him on the cheek. He was surprised but he hugged me back.

It's funny because I wasn't sure what would happen and really nothing did but when I let go of him he looked at me strangely like he was seeing me for the first time. I smiled and asked if he was okay and he just nodded. I asked him if he wanted the money and he just nodded again. I got the money from the kitchen drawer. There was £800 which was half of what I had earned, plus the extra £250. Yuri took the money and I asked him if he wanted to go into the bedroom and he said yes. We went into the bedroom and we had sex but he wasn't as rough as he had been before and afterwards he asked me where I am from.

Everything I told him was a lie. I told him I didn't have any children and that my family was from Phuket. Nothing I told him was the truth. He told me that he had three brothers and one sister and that his father had died when he was a small boy but really I didn't care about him or his family at all. I could see that Yuri had changed and I am sure it was the perfume that had changed him He didn't have the same look in his eye that Simon or Robert has, but I could see that he wanted me. But not like he wanted me before. Before he wanted to hurt me and to have power over me, but now he cares about me. He still wants to have sex with me but now he doesn't want to hurt me. I asked him if I could have his phone number and I said yes. Then I gave him a sexy massage and while I was doing that I started asking him questions about Sacha and while I asked the questions I made sure that he was hard and then I had sex with him.

He told me that Sacha's name wasn't really Sacha. It was Jonas. And do you know, Oliver wasn't Oliver's real name either. It was Lam. All the time I had known Oliver he had been lying to me. When Yuri went he was still looking at me strangely and I knew then for sure that the perfume had done what Bee had said it would do. Before I wasn't sure about Laos magic but now I believe that it works.

The next thing I had to do was to talk to Candy. Candy is strong. That is why she does domination, I am sure. I knew she would help me and that she would be strong. I didn't want to tell anyone else because if I told too many people what I wanted to do then it would go wrong and I definitely didn't want it to go wrong.

The next day Yuri came around to get my money but I could tell that he wanted sex so we had sex first and again he wasn't so rough with me. He wanted to know the story of my life so I lied to him and said that my father was dead and that my mother was sick which is why I'm doing this job. He said that he didn't like me doing this job which was a strange thing to say because he is mafia and he works for Sacha who is making me do this job so then I knew that I could easily get Yuri to do anything that I wanted.

I was still getting a lot of customers, but it didn't seem so bad because I had a plan. Natalie sent us customers on Saturday afternoon even though we had to go to the party at the house in St John's Wood. The house was Sacha's, Yuri told me that. And he said that Sacha kept a lot of money in a safe in one of the bedrooms, in the back of a wardrobe. Yuri said that he didn't know the combination because Sacha didn't trust anybody. But he said that often Sacha just left money in a cupboard in his study. And Yuri said that there were lots of guns in the house. Sacha liked guns. Yuri was giving me a lot of information because he liked to talk to me. He told me lots of things but everything I told him was a lie.

I did not feel bad about lying to Yuri. He was not being nice to me because he is *Jai Dee*, he was being nice to me because Bee's perfume had worked. I talked to Yuri about Sacha, and what a bad man Sacha was. I told Yuri that Sacha sometimes made me have sex with him. I told Yuri that Sacha was causing too much trouble and that maybe one day the police would catch him. And I told Yuri that Sacha said bad things about Yuri, that he didn't trust him and that one day he would do something bad to Yuri.

I could see that Yuri believed everything that I told him. I think that is because of the magic perfume, but also because Yuri is quite stupid. And also I think that everyone who works for Sacha knows that he is a bad man and that he does not stay loyal to his friends. Oliver Was supposed to be his friend, but Sacha took the agency from him. So it was easy for Yuri to believe me. The Thais have an expression for it - *Pak Waan*. It means sweet mouth. It is a way of talking to someone so that it makes them feel good. That is what I did to Yuri. I talked to him with a sweet mouth. I told him that the girls would be happier if he was the boss. That he would be a better boss than Sacha.

We went to the party at the house in St John's Wood. I had to do the domination show with Dao and Candy. They both whipped me and I had to do oral on them both and then Dao put on a strap-on and made love to me and she was quite rough, as if she enjoyed hurting me.

Everyone was drinking champagne and taking drugs and like before the agency girls all had to dress like prostitutes while the men all had on suits and the girls with them had sexy dresses. It's like we were animals to amuse them, that's how they treated us. Dao stayed near to Sacha and I could see from the way that Sacha was looking at her that the perfume had worked on him. I don't think Dao understands what has happened, though. I think if she knew how powerful Bee's perfume was then she would start to get Sacha to do whatever she wanted.

Nancy was really unhappy because she didn't want to have sex now because she now wanted to keep the baby. I found her crying in one of the bedrooms because three men had had sex with her and now she was hurting inside and there was blood on the sheets. I told her not to worry, that everything was going to be okay, but she just said that she wanted to kill herself. I held her hands and swore to her that I would take care of her and she nodded and then I made her promise that she wouldn't try to kill herself again.

The party finished at six o'clock in the morning. Nancy wanted to go home with me but I said that Yuri wanted to take me to his home. She was a bit sad about that but she went home in an Uber taxi with Dao and Wanda.

When Yuri and I left the party there was only Sacha and three other men in the house. One of them wanted me to give him oral before I went but Yuri said he was taking me back home to have sex with me. Sacha said that I should get some sleep because tomorrow I would be working and I just smiled because I knew that I would never be working again.

I put some more perfume on as we walked to Yuri's car. It was a big BMW, black with tinted windows. I got into his car and we drove away from the house, but he stopped the car down the road. We sat in the car and waited until the three men had gone and Sacha was alone in the house. Then I kissed Yuri and said that it was time and he knew what he had to do and he nodded and said yes, he knew.

He got out of the car and blew me a kiss and then he went over to the gate and pressed the intercom and after a while the gates opened. I sat in the car and waited. I didn't hear any noise from inside the house but I knew what was happening. Five minutes later Yuri came back, carrying a large bag. He was breathing really heavily and his eyes were hard like glass. I asked him if everything was okay and he nodded. I asked him what he'd done with the gun and he said he'd left it next to the body and that he'd wiped the fingerprints off it. The gun was one of Sacha's. Yuri had done exactly what I had told him. He had told Sacha that he needed to talk to him and Sacha had given him some champagne and then Yuri had said that he needed to use the toilet and then he had gone to get one of Sacha's guns and then he had shot him twice, once in the head and once the chest, using a pillow to keep the gun quiet.

I took the bag off him and opened it. It was full of money. I asked him how much and he said he didn't know but he thought there was probably at least three hundred thousand pounds. Then he gave me the passports and ID cards of all the girls in the agency. I said he had done well and he kissed me and he said that he wanted to make love to me in the car but I said we should go home first. He drove me back to his house which was in Ealing in West London. It was a small house but quite nice. As soon as we were inside he wanted to make love to me but I said we should do it in the bedroom and that we should drink some wine to celebrate. And I said he should shower and put his clothes in a bag so that we could take them to be dry cleaned to get rid of any evidence and he said I was a smart girl and I said I knew I was and kissed him. He went upstairs while I went into the kitchen to get him some wine.

When I went upstairs with two glasses of wine he had showered and was lying on the bed. He asked me if I loved him and I lied and said I did. *Pak Waan*. I kissed him and I gave him his wine and then we clinked glasses and we both drank. He said that he loved me and that he had done what he had done for me and I said I knew and I kissed him again. He finished his wine and then he started making love to me. I said he should lie on his back and he did and I made love to him very slowly and his eyes closed and then he started snoring. He was asleep. I had put four tablets into the wine. I had ground them into a powder in my flat and it was easy to dissolve them in the wine. I pinched him but he didn't wake up.

Then I phoned Candy and waited for her to come to Yuri's house. It took her thirty minutes to get there and I sat watching Yuri while I waited. He snored a lot. He was in a deep sleep.

When Candy came she brought the gun that Yuri had used to kill Sacha. That was our plan. Candy had hidden in the house after the party. She had stayed in a wardrobe and kept quiet while Yuri had killed Sacha and taken his money and the passports. Yuri had wiped his fingerprints off the gun and left it next to Sacha's body. But what he didn't know was that Candy was still in the house. She picked up the gun and she put it in her bag and she brought it to Yuri's house. Candy brought a carrier bag with her and in the bag were two pairs of the long black leather gloves that she uses for domination. We put on the gloves and then we wiped everywhere clean so that no one would know that we had been there. I cleaned the wine glasses and put one of them away. I put one glass in Yuri's hand to get his fingerprints on it and then put some wine in it and put it next to the bed. Then we put the gun in Yuri's hand to get his fingerprints on it, and then we hid it under the bed.

Candy and I wiped everything that we had touched. Then we started laughing because we knew that everything was going to be okay. I showed Candy the money and she screamed and hugged me and kissed me. We both jumped up and down with joy because we were rich and because Sacha could never hurt us or our families again. And I gave her back her passport and ID card, and the passports and ID cards of all the girls.

We left the house and as we were walking down the road I phoned Neil, the policeman who worked for the Human Trafficking Command. I changed my voice a bit when I spoke to him but I don't think I needed to because I am sure he speaks to many Asian girls. He sounded sleepy so I spoke slowly to make sure that he had understood. I told him that Yuri had killed Sacha and that Sacha's real name was Jonas and I told him where Yuri lived. He asked me who I was but I switched off the phone and broke the SIM card in half and threw it away.

I was sure that Neil would go to Yuri's house and the police would find Yuri asleep. Then they would find the gun and they would find his clothes and they would test them and find out that Yuri had fired the gun. There is nothing that Yuri could say because really he did kill Sacha. He would have been surprised when the police had told him that the gun had his fingerprints on it but he wouldn't have been able to do anything.

Candy and I walked a long way from Yuri's house before we took a taxi back to my apartment. We were carrying the money that Yuri had taken from Sacha. It was a fortune. There was actually three hundred and twenty thousand pounds. We split it up afterwards. We gave fifty thousand pounds to Nancy and Candy and I had one hundred and thirty five pounds each. That is enough money for me and Ice to live on for a long, long time. Maybe for ever.

I didn't think it was a good idea to put the money in a suitcase when I flew to Thailand so I asked Vince to help me and he did. He used his Smurfs to put the money into his accounts and then he transferred it to my bank account in Udon Thani and he didn't charge me a commission or anything, which is nice. Vince said that one day he might come out to Thailand for a holiday and I said he could come and stay at my house.

I don't take cocaine any more. I have lots of energy, and my life is perfect. The only thing I don't have yet is a man who loves me and my son but I think I will meet someone. I hope so. But I am sure of one thing. I want him to love me for myself and not because I have used Bee's magic perfume. I want the love to be real, and I want my husband whoever he is to love me because he loves me and wants to take care of me. I still have the perfume, though. Just in case.

Printed in Great Britain
by Amazon

59184257R00130